Stake Sandwich

ANNALEE ADAMS

Congratulations
&
Happy reading!
♡ Mele

STAKE SANDWICH

First edition. January 2022.
Copyright © 2022 Annalee Adams.
The moral rights of the author have been asserted.
Written by Annalee Adams.
This is a work of fiction. Similarities to real people, places, or events are entirely coincidental.
All rights reserved.
No part of this publication may be reproduced, transmitted, or stored in a retrieval system in any form or by any other means, without prior written permission from the author, Annalee Adams. No part of this publication may be circulated in any form of binding or cover than that which it is published in.
ISBN: 979-8-76-2347952
This book has been typeset in Garamond.
www.AnnaleeAdams.com

To everyone that dreams of a world beyond their own.

Other books by Annalee Adams

In this universe:

The Resurgence series:
Dark Truth (2022)
Dark Phoenix (2022)

The Fire Wolf Prophecies:
Crimson Bride (2022)
Crimson Army (2022)

The Shop Series:
Stake Sandwich
The Devil Made Me Do It (July 2022)
Strawberry Daiquiri Desire (December 2022)

Other books not in this universe:

The Celestial Rose Series:
Eternal Entity
Eternal Creation
Eternal Devastation
Eternal Ending

Gretel

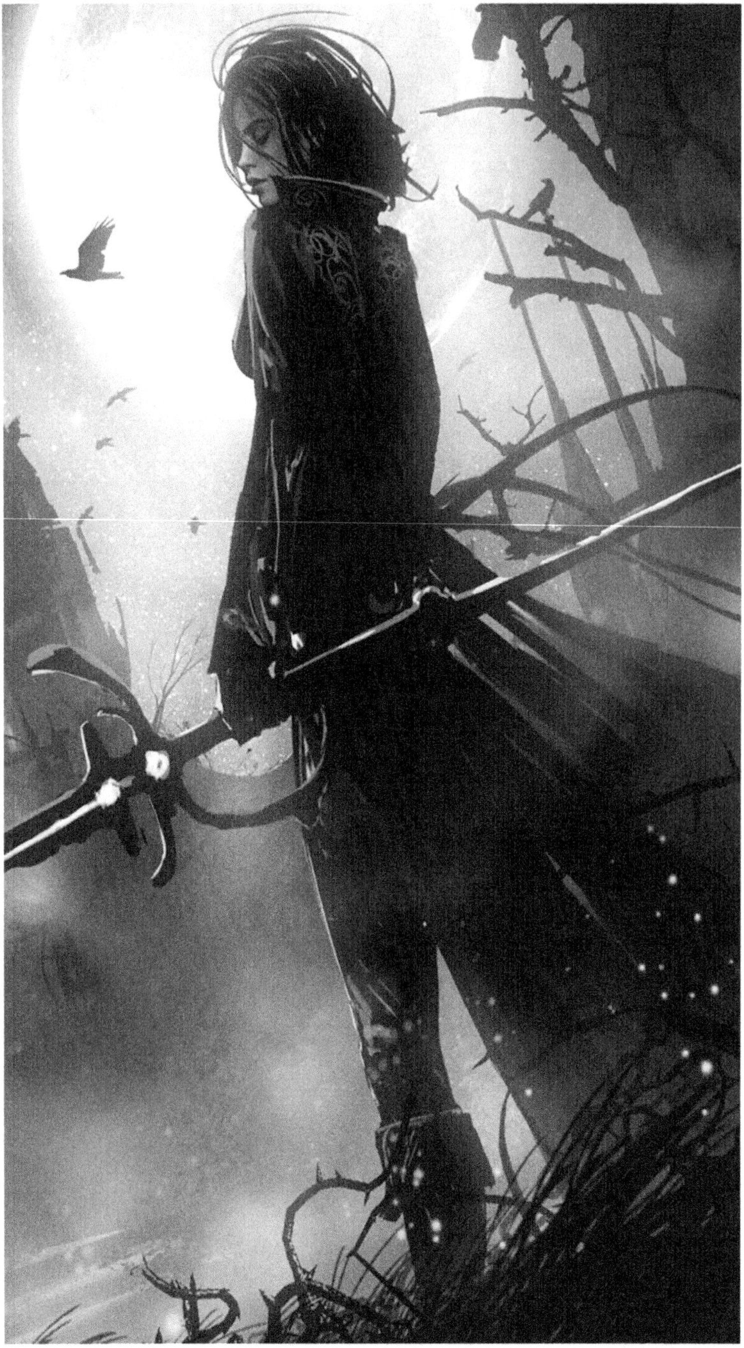

CHAPTER ONE

A motionless corpse is a good corpse. It's when they jump up and chow down for a bite you should worry.

Being a vampire hunter isn't all it's made out to be. There's the extra strength and agility. But the downside is you get hit on every night by some creep in a dark alley.

Tonight isn't any different, it's Saturday, and in Los Angeles, that means one thing; Strauss is out picking off his weekly victims. I have tracked him so far, but somehow, things got turned around and now, I am the prey. I'd like to say it was planned… but who am I kidding!

Slithering through the darkness, he crept. Scouring the town for his next victim. Shadows cradled his figure as he licked his lips in anticipation. Every soul is a target, every neck a scrumptious meal. I shuddered at the thought of it. Strauss.

The be all and end all of immortality. I'd watched him for days, weeks, in fact. I knew his every move, his usual haunts, and every victim he had taken.

My mum said research was a girl's best friend. She's right. Because of my surveillance, I now know that every Friday at 10pm; he's outside Club Neo, stalking his next victim.

I'm Layla, Layla Stone. I'm a born and bred hunter. Exceptionally strong, perfectly agile, and damned well confident. I've been fighting vampires ever since my best friend Natasha had been kissing them. Yes. That's actually true. Her first kiss was with a vampire. I smirked. Lucky for her, I saved her ass that night. Not that she'll ever know!

Dad said it's in our blood. We're born hunters. One of five families here in LA that were put on this Earth to level the playing field. It's our gift, or our curse. I'm yet to decide which.

Over the last century, our family has hunted the original vampires. There are six in total. But Strauss is the one we are training to take down. He's the militant, the trickster, the player, and the fool. He's sick in the head, enjoying body mutilation, carving up his victims and watching them bleed out.

Strauss recently resurfaced near the pier in Santa Monica, on the westside of LA. We were on one of our patrols when we came across his calling card, a pile of corpses with a carved rose engraved into their skin. It would be humorous if it weren't horrific.

So tonight, I tracked him, right here to this alleyway. The fact that I've found him, and I'm alone should worry me. But it doesn't. I trust my instincts, and my training. I know I can beat him. I have to. He has to pay for killing my brother, and every other victim he's taken.

My parents warned me. Told me to step back and stay in the shadows. They wanted me to watch, not engage. The problem is, I'm pretty sure he already knows I'm here. He would have caught my scent a mile ago. Over the last hour he's played me, sending me in circles, until we ended up right here, in this dead-end alleyway. I'm screwed!

The last time he visited LA was six years ago. The night my older brother Timmy was murdered. Even with all the training Timmy had, he never saw Strauss coming. Timmy's the reason Strauss is our number one target. He's the reason we fight the good fight and will one day avenge his death. I sighed. I missed my big brother.

Dad said I should concentrate on school. He said to leave the heroics to the heroes. But I can be a hero too. Granted, I'm only seventeen and at college, but I'm a lot stronger than most hunters out there.

Every night we take turns on patrol, tracking him. Him and his followers. His latest victim was an 18-year-old with an attitude. The recently dead girl was a rising star in the drama community. I shrugged, taking out my dagger as it gleamed in the moonlight. I know I should feel guilty. But I don't. I can't save them all. But what I can do is save his next target, especially now I know where he takes them from.

So, tonight is the night! I know he's waiting somewhere

deep in the shadows. He's ready to make me his next victim. I smirked. He'll get a fright when he tries to take me down. My eyes widened as I checked out every darkened crevice, shuddering as an icy chill blasted past me. Okay, so I'm not a total idiot. I know full well I'll be in for quite the fight if Strauss shows up. I need backup. Picking up my phone, I texted my dad again.

A few minutes passed, but there was no reply. *Shit! I'm screwed!* I gulped. Shadows swayed around me, the darkened figure of a man stepped out, his laughter curdling the airwaves. Arming myself, I was ready to fight.

My hand grabbed the hilt of my dagger. Nothing. Nothing walked out. Am I seeing things? Then again, I know vampires can speed past you in a flash of light. Maybe the figure in the darkness was the wind? Maybe he ran away, scared for his life? I laughed, smugly.

I'd like to believe that's what he did. But you don't get to be an original vampire if you run away from every battle. My phone buzzed. Thank god! I picked it up. A spam message came through. Bloody hell! Where's Dad? He must be in the middle of something.

Tonight, Dad was on the hunt with JimBob. I smiled. JimBob's only human, and to be quite honest, Dad just liked the company. We took him on at our local sandwich shop about a year ago. But ever since his sister was slaughtered; by one of the local vampire gangs, we've had to babysit him. It's not that he's frightened. No. Quite the opposite. The problem is, JimBob wants to dive in and destroy every one of the bloodsucking fiends. I'll give him that. He has some balls. But those balls will get him killed. Dad is quite fond of him. He respects his desire to kill every beast with two fangs and no heartbeat. I like him too. After all, he is the only friend that I can be honest with.

So, after Jessie was murdered; JimBob's younger sister. He quickly realized the whole supernatural world was real, and that we were keeping the monsters at bay.

Shadows darted across the alleyway as a drunk boy came stumbling out. He headed right for me, then barfed in the corner. Gross.

Standing there, I kept my back to the wall. Thinking back, I remember the realization when the shit hits the fan, and for the first time, you can see the supernatural world around you. Reality comes crashing down. I sighed. It's tough. I knew nothing about monsters and demons until I reached puberty. Thirteen, in fact. It wasn't a pretty sight.

When reality smacked me hard in the face, I trained. After learning the truth behind Timmy's death, I needed to ensure I was ready to avenge him once and for all. So that's why I'm here in this dive of an alleyway.

Scrunching up my nose, I backed away from the bins, watching as the drunken boy child left. The local law enforcement had cordoned off the alleyway, because of last week's bloodless corpse. I smirked at the ripped police tape as it rode on the shrill of the wind, carrying my scent up and out of the alleyway. If Strauss didn't know before, he knew now.

I stood there, prey to a predator, an easy target, offered out on a silver platter. I yawned, straining to keep my eyes open. *It's getting late. Where is he?* The stench of the skip drifted past me. I made a face. *It's disgusting. I've had some bad gigs in my time, but this one has got to be the worst!*

Next to the skip, the back door of the nightclub remained open. Rock music continued to blare, and three civilians stumbled out, giggling. The man entered the alleyway first, biting down on a greasy burger. Followed by two slim, bubbly blond girls that towered above him, swaying, enjoying his attention. His wiry beard made him look older than the girls, early twenties perhaps. I shrugged. *Either way, he must have a lot of money, as there's no way he could pull those two without it.* They stopped, standing in the center of my kill zone. *Shit.*

"Don't you think you ought to get them home?" I said, leaning against the wall.

The man turned, leering. I swallowed back bile at the sight of him. *Burgh! What a creep.* The girls held onto each of his arms, giggling.

"Don't you think you ought to mind your own business?"

Out of the shadows, a cackle of laughter blasted over the airwaves. A young, suited man with blond hair, dark eyes and an average figure stepped out. "Now that's no way to speak to a lady," he said, his eyes taking in the situation.

Oh shit!

CHAPTER TWO

Shit. Strauss, it has to be. I stood tall, withdrew my weapon and yelled to the drunken party, "Get out. Get out now."

Within a millisecond, Strauss sped past me. He took the bearded man in his arms, crushing his head; grinding and cracking his skull, his eyes popping out as it flattened. Blood spurted everywhere, covering the girls like something out of Carrie. Screaming, the girls ran off, leaving a lone half-eaten burger beside their dead friend's body. Strauss grinned, wiping his hands on a handkerchief.

I leapt forward, dagger at the ready, running and jumping on his back. Twisting myself around, bringing my blade to his ice-cold neck.

"Oh, you like to get right down to business, don't you?"

At a break-neck speed he spun, launching me across the alleyway; landing smack bang in the middle of blood and vomit; dazed. I gagged a few times; the stench was breathtaking.

Callous laughter emanated behind me, growing closer by the second. Hands reached down, grabbing me by the scruff of my neck, throwing me into the air. My eyesight faltered. Speckles of black, white, and gray corroded my vision. It was too fast. Too soon. As my ragdoll body came to a thundering halt, he punched me down hard, impaling my chest with his fist. All remaining breath ripped out of me as I hurtled forward, crashing into the skip.

Coughing blood, I gasped for air. Broken ribs crying out in pain as my connective tissue sought to knit itself back together. Another bonus of being a hunter, faster healing. The problem was, healing required energy, and after that failure of a battle, I was running on empty.

I lay broken and bloody on the cold, hard ground. *Shit. Don't pass out!* My vision blackened; perspective blurred. He smirked as he sped over. His deadly teeth bared out before me. I could feel his thick, brutish arms as he pulled me up. His head lowered. Sharpened fangs glistening in the moonlight. Leaning down he brushed my hair off my delicate neck and readied himself to take the bite that would end my mortal existence on this earth.

This was the moment I had waited for. After Timmy died, I vowed to use my hunter's gift for good. I had to avenge his death. But now, it looked like I wouldn't be avenging him. I'd be joining him. Taking a deep breath, I waited for the intensity of his fangs slicing into my carotid. I should have left, and waited for backup. But no, I had to play the hero, saving the next person from slaughter.

I never stood a chance. Strauss was more powerful than I ever imagined! The fact my body hadn't snapped in two when he threw me against the skip was purely down to my hunter genes.

As I braced myself for his bite, a dark-haired man sped through the alleyway, landing smack bang in the middle of us. The mystery man's gorgeous face was the last thing I saw before I was thrown, free floating in the air.

I didn't land. Instead, I fell into his arms. Silvered eyes looking down at me. *Who or what is he?* His strained face is a picture of emotion; the longing, the sadness, and solace. Carrying me, he kept me close, his icy chest penetrating my clothing, shivers protruding my body.

I don't know why he saved me, or what he is; but he shares the same traits as a vampire. It doesn't make sense; no vampire would help me. No undead creature would risk their own immortality to save the very being that hunts them.

As we sped away, I reached upwards. I could feel the softness of his hair. Thick, long, dark hair, covering his pale ice-cold face. Soft pink lips smiled, as his sharpened fangs threatened my life. My eyes widened. There is nothing I can do. I'm a slave to his needs. My body is broken, my mind a mess of dazed confusion. Even if I want to, I can't see well enough to be any match for a vampire right now.

He brushed his icy fingers over my battered cheekbone. *He cares. Why does he care?* His irises swirled, silvers and gray intertwined with a touch of oceanic blue. *Who is he?* Dropping my arm, I relaxed into his chest.

He has the same strength I do. The same agility. But he isn't like me. Nothing like me. For starters, he's ice cold with no heart beating in his chest. This savior of mine is a cold dead vampire, and I don't know why but he risked everything to help me.

A moment later, we came to an abrupt halt. I was outside my house. Resting me down on the swing seat, he covered me over with a blanket. My body ached, otherwise I would have jumped up, standing my ground. But then, I'm sure I've broken at least a few bones, because my god it hurt. It will heal, it always does. I just hope I heal quick enough to take down that son of a bitch. Strauss had it coming, and next time I'm bringing the whole five families down on his ass.

The strangely handsome vampire stood above me, looking down. "Who are you?" I asked, looking up at him. He smiled, his razor-sharp fangs glinting in the moonlight. Stepping back, he banged on the door, left, and fled into the darkness of the night. Leaving me as the door opened, and my parents carried me to safety.

That night, I dreamt of a man, the man that saved me.

Darkness shrouded him. But in my dreams, he wasn't a man; he's much more.

With silvered fangs, enchanting silvery blue eyes, and a face as pale as snow. He was frozen in time; the world moving on without him. His long, dark hair curtained his icy features as he carried me home. His solemn face enthralled me. Pain encircled his eyes. But no matter how tortured he was, he was still a corpse, a dead man walking; and if you ask him what he eats to survive, his answer will be the blood of the innocent, and that is the reason he has to die…. Again.

The problem is, with every fiber of my being, I know I won't be able to stake him. It feels wrong to consider him as evil. He is nothing like Strauss or the other vampires. He seems much more than that.

My dreams warped and changed, the fight played back, and I saw myself broken and bloodied. He came at the right time, but why? Why would something so evil have any ounce of humanity left in his timeless body? His lust for blood alone should have led him to ravish me. But instead, he risked his own immortality in a fight against an original vampire; to save a girl that hunted his kind for a living. It made no sense.

I had told my parents what happened. It confused them as much as it did me. But Dad said what's dead is dead, and it should remain so.

I sighed, tossing and turning. I wonder how many innocent humans; my savior had killed. How many more would take their last breath because of him. Even though he saved me, he was still built to be a monster. None of it made sense.

He showed remorse, and with me, he seemed to care. That instinct alone went against his carnivorous nature. A vampire with feelings was unheard of, and I'd know. I had studied all the books on supernatural creatures.

So, what is he then?

CHAPTER THREE

The next morning, I woke up with a start, jumping up, stake in hand. I must have dreamt of Strauss; dreamt of the complete mess I had made of the battle.

Yawning, I stretched my arms over my head, gazing out at the rays of sunlight as they cast their light through the window.

It's Sunday morning, and any normal person would still be in bed at this god-earthly hour. I had time off from college, no patrol duty, and only had to help at the sandwich shop for a few hours this afternoon. Plus, I had received an invitation. Natasha, one of my closest 'normal' friends, had invited me to a party at her house. Sighing, I got up, pulled open my wardrobe doors, and inspected the lack of 'pretty' outfits I had. Most of it was black, inconspicuous, and deadly. Mum had sewn secret pockets in most of my clothes, perfect for a mini stake or two.

I smiled.

Even if I'm not the social cheerleader, I make myself out to be, there is one particular reason I want to go. Lucas is going to be there. The hot-headed, gorgeous, star quarterback everyone loves and adores. He was the reason our college reached the finals last month. I smiled as I flicked through my clothes. I'd often see him at practice. He loved to stand and pose, showing off his biceps for all the fragile giggly girls out there. Heck, half the cheer squad was Lucas's own personal fan club. Not me though. I knew he was an idiot. But I would happily stand back and admire that tight arse of his any day. I laughed to myself.

Maybe a party is everything I need right now, some kind of normality to escape the messed-up world we lived in. It was hard to go to college, sit around and study, knowing full well the supernatural realm lived amongst us.

I closed the wardrobe and headed into the shower. Damn, it was cold. It always was to start with. Mum said we needed to save money. After all, we weren't paid to be hunters. The sandwich shop was all we had, and that hardly covered the bills every month.

A few minutes later, I had scrubbed my body, and washed my dark blond hair. Jumping out, frozen to the core. I padded across my dark blue carpet and pulled on a pair of jeans, tee-shirt and jumper. Running a hairbrush through the knots, I tied my hair back. Gazing in the mirror, my reflection showed a tired, dark-circled pale face. I groaned and applied a tinted moisturizer, concealer, and lip balm. Finally, I was ready to go, and by the sounds of it, mum and dad had already left for the early shift at the sandwich shop.

I walked downstairs and grabbed a slice of toast from our outdated kitchen. JimBob would be on shift with me this afternoon, and I know full well he'd have a trillion questions to ask me. It was hard keeping him quiet, especially when he was serving customers. I mean, the amount of people that must have thought he was loony amazed me. But he didn't care. I think, like us, he was obsessed with the undead and the darkness of the world; but then again, what teenager wasn't.

My parents are going to meet the heads of each family later today. The five families this side of LA group together and help each other out. They meet every month below the library off of the Old Mill estate; and I could guess what today's topic of choice will be; my mystery guest from last night.

Years ago, when we moved to LA, we needed a front. Mum came up with the shop idea. It was genius really. A quick and easy business to run; and we got to know the gossip in the local area. Plus, the Gothic decor was a hit with the kids, and at least it was somewhere they could come and be safe. It was better than hanging out on street corners or by bus stops as open targets for the predators of the night.

Mum enjoyed honing the menu into a parade of hunters' delights. She purposely served anything and everything that took the piss out of the undead. Blood Soup, Death by Slayer, Stake Sandwich, to name a few. Heck, the entire shop was a vampire hunter's paradise. We displayed weapons all over the place. The local kids loved it, and thought it was quirky. I smirked. At least it kept the vampires away.

Finishing my breakfast, I cleaned up, wrapped up warmly, and headed out to the shop. It was cold outside; the wind was picking up speed; tonight would be a tough one. Luckily, I wasn't on patrol tonight. It was one of the other families' turns. Heading past the park, I shuddered. The whole place creeps me out. It had had its fair share of vampire sightings over the last few weeks. Maybe I'll head there to take my anger out on the world. I sighed, shaking my head. I was still pissed that I screwed up with Strauss.

Two blocks later, I arrived, and by looking at the queue going out the door, I was just in time for the afternoon lunch rush. I rolled my eyes. *Great*.

As I arrived, the thick glass door swayed under the stormy winds of Winter's reign. It was cold outside, too bloody cold. I shuddered, closing the door behind me.

JimBob waved and continued to serve one of the skater lads from Harp Alley. They were the usual midday crowd, every Saturday afternoon. They looked scary to the average human, but even with all the piercings, long hair, and baggy trousers, they weren't. In fact, Gill was one of the kindest kids I knew, and the local runner for Chase Bradley's gang. I rolled my eyes, spying his cronies sitting in the corner booth. JimBob smirked.

Taking off my coat, I went into the back, then through into the kitchen. Mum stood preparing a selection of sandwiches, while in the middle of a video call with Dad about my sexy savior. She silenced when she saw me. "Hi Layla," she said.

"Hey Pumpkin," Dad said over the speaker.

"Hi Mum. Dad, where are you?"

"He's setting up for today's meeting honey."

"I'm here," Dad said. I nodded, walking over, and waving to him over the phone.

"So, are you heading out too?" I asked my Mum.

"Yes, as soon as I've finished these."

I nodded. "I'll finish them," I said.

Mum smiled, placing down the butter knife. "Thanks honey."

I washed my hands and continued to spread the cheap mayonnaise on all the sandwiches. It smelt disgusting, but all the kids liked it. Mum grabbed her coat, pulled on her hat, and wrapped up warmly for her journey into the icy world outside. She was still chatting to Dad on the video call.

"Make sure you tell her," Dad said. She nodded, walking back into the kitchen.

"Tell me what?" I asked. Mum sighed. She turned the phone to me so I could see Dad on camera.

"Hey Pumpkin."

"Hi Dad, what's up?"

"I need you to come straight home tonight."

"Why?"

Mum huffed. "Because Strauss has your scent now, he will

track you."

"Shit."

"Language!" Mum said. I groaned.

"Can I stop by the gym on the way?"

"What alone?" Mum said.

"No, I'll take JimBob."

Dad sighed. "JimBob's not a hunter pumpkin."

"Yes, I know, but safety in numbers. Besides, Strauss usually anchors down until Saturday night."

Mum nodded. "She has a point."

"Fine," Dad said. "But any trouble and you call us."

"I will do."

"And stay away from that vampire from last night."

"What the one that saved me?"

"Yes honey," Mum said. "Just because he saved you once, doesn't mean he won't hurt you next time."

"Listen to your mother pumpkin, she's usually right."

Mum smiled. "Always right, don't you mean?" Dad laughed, and I smirked.

"Fine," Dad said. "But stay away from him. We don't know his intentions yet."

"I know, but don't you think if he wanted to hurt me, he would have when he had ample opportunity last night?"

"Yes, but how did he know where you lived?"

I frowned. "I, err, I don't know."

"Exactly," Dad said. "He must have been stalking you for quite some time."

"But why?"

"That's the point honey," Mum said. "We don't know enough about him yet. What if he's working for Strauss?"

"Then he'd have helped him kill me… surely?"

Dad sighed. "You know Strauss likes to play tricks… he enjoys the hunt."

"Yes," I groaned. "I know."

"And what do I always say pumpkin?"

"What's dead should stay dead, Dad. We can't trust vampires."

"That's right, now heed that advice and tell us if you see him again."

"Fine." I huffed. "I will do."

Dad nodded. Mum smiled and kissed my forehead. "I'll see you later," she said.

"Yep, see you both later."

I know they have a point, and I've never met a vampire that isn't anything but bloodthirsty, vicious, and dead. But there was something different about him. I sighed. What if they are right?

CHAPTER FOUR

Ah well, best get on sorting these sandwiches. I watched as Mum left with Dad still chatting away on the video call. I smirked. It was amazing to see old people with new technology.

Mum and Dad were both aged fifty, born with the same hunter gene, although they came from two separate families. Dad was originally from the Stone family, and mum came from the Raydon side.

Because of our line of work, it was normal for one person to marry into another hunter's family. I sulked. The problem with that was, the only other boy about my age was Dylan Rose; an obnoxious, arrogant prick of a boy. I would never let it happen, even if my parents willed it so. Thus, I'd decided early on that I'd remain single, unless I married into another family from another state. I shrugged.

Marriage should be the last thing on my mind right now. After all, as soon as you reached twenty-one, it was expected that you marry and birth the next generation, securing the hunter gene. The whole thing was messed up in my eyes, but thankfully I had a few more years until that was demanded of me.

I finished the sandwiches, placed them on a tray and took them through to the shop. JimBob smiled, then continued serving a couple I recognised from college. I waved and smiled at them.

Just as I always did, wave and smile, wave, and smile. It always amazed me how little of the world humanity actually knew. They sit there with their lattes, ordering quirky sandwiches and cakes, and are blind to the fucked-up world we lived in. I sighed. At least they can sleep at night. They'll never know the truth.

Jim Bob knew that the whole sandwich shop was a pastel idiocy, designed to pull in clientele, but quirky enough to save our asses should vampires come out to play.

My parents thought it'd be amusing to play on the whole supernatural theme. A few runic symbols scored into the woodwork, and we were safe from most of the demonic realm. Besides our home, this is the safest place any human could be. Dad says it's best to keep the demons away, then have them come out to play. It made sense.

Looking at the menu board, I saw mum had made her speciality of the day, her favorite sandwich, the Stake Sandwich.

I smirked. It was, after all, pretty damn amusing. She loved to taunt them, taking the piss out of vampires whenever she could. She'd even drawn a bloody steak sandwich with an actual wooden stake coming out of it on the menu board. Brilliant!

The till dinged as JimBob took money from the couple from college. He thanked them and walked over to me. "Hi Layla. How's it hanging?" I smiled. He was sweet, but really weird.

"I'm good thanks JimBob, how are you doing?"

"Much better now I've been out with your dad." I nodded. "We actually took one down the other night. Your Dad's brilliant!" I smiled. When hunting, my dad was pretty brilliant. "So, I want in on the whole hunting thing."

"What do you mean?"

"Your Dad said you were bloody fast, and stronger than him."

I laughed. "That's 'cos he's old."

He smirked. "True dat, but he said you could teach me."

I rolled my eyes. "He did, did he?"

JimBob nodded. "Like I know, I'm never going to be as strong as a hunter. But I can train and help, can't I?"

"I, erm, I don't know. It's pretty dangerous out there."

"Yeah, I know. But I can't just stand here serving sandwiches all my life. I've got to do something Layla. I have to avenge her death."

I sighed. "I know JimBob."

"So, what do you think?" he asked, his eyes pleading with me.

"Fine. I can train you. But if you get yourself killed, that's on you, okay?" I smirked.

He jumped up, and fist bumped the air. "Thank you! Thank you!" he came over and hugged me. I remain stiff, prising myself away from him. He really needed to shower.

"So, are you hunting tonight?" he asked, rather too loudly.

"Shhh," I said.

"Oh," he pretended to zip his mouth shut. "So, are you?" he whispered.

"No. Dad wants me home asap."

"Oh," he looked saddened by this.

I groaned. "But he said I could go to the gym. I can start your training there?"

"Yay!" he jumped up and fist-bumped the air. Grinning as wide as a Cheshire Cat.

I chuckled. "It's best we start in the gym. There's no way I can keep you safe out there at night. Not right now."

He nodded. "I heard about last night."

"Yeah. I was bloody lucky that another vamp was nearby."

His mouth fell open. "A vampire, really? He saved you?"

I nodded. He shook his head, then playfully hit me on the shoulder.

I laughed. "I'm being serious."

His eyes widened. "But a vampire?"

"Yeah, I'm as shocked as you."

"Why though? Why would he save you?"

Hesitating, I said, "that's the worrying thing, I don't know why."

Jeremy, from my sports class, walked up to the counter. "Hi Layla,"

I coughed, took a deep breath, and turned to face him. "Hi"

"So, are you going to that party tonight?"

I groaned. Shit. I'd forgotten about that.

"Party?" JimBob said.

Jeremy looked at him and frowned. "Yeah, there's a get together over at Natasha's."

"Oh."

"You can come too, if you bring Layla along." Jeremy said. I shuddered. He had always been a bit of a creep.

"Definitely… right Layla?" JimBob said.

I groaned. "Yes, of course," I said. Reminding myself to smile and wave, smile, and wave. Acting 'normal' is bloody hard these days.

JimBob smiled and took Jeremy's order. Two Stake Sandwiches. I grinned, getting them ready.

The rest of the shift was much the same. We'd sold out of our speciality sandwich and almost finished all the Bloody Devil Cakes too. Luckily for us, when it came to closing time, there were two slices left.

JimBob and I cleaned up, sat down, and devoured the cake before us.

"Your Mum makes a mean cake."

I smiled. "She sure does."

"So, what's the plan, then?"

"Well, we're going to have to go to the gym later tonight, as you accepted the party invite," I said, grinning.

JimBob's eyes widened. "Wait. What. Didn't you want to go?"

I laughed. "Yeah, I'd just forgotten."

"Phew!"

"So, meet at mine in an hour?" I said. He nodded. We closed up, both went our separate ways and changed ready for the party.

CHAPTER FIVE

Back home I was as ready as I ever would be. The doorbell rang and I shouted for JimBob to come in. As I stepped downstairs, I could see him chatting with my dad.

"Are you ready?" dad said, jingling his keys.

I nodded, grabbed my coat, and got in dads' car. JimBob sat there grinning. He looked much the same as earlier, except the top. This one was another ripped old band shirt. I smiled.

JimBob was studying the arts. He's the creative type and loves to sculpt weird and wonderful things. To be fair, the whole world of vampires and demons suits him. If only he had the strength and agility to go with it. I smiled. I could see JimBob making a brilliant hunter. I just hoped I wouldn't get him killed in the process.

Dad dropped us off at Natasha's, we thanked him and walked up the path. JimBob took a long, deep sigh. "What's wrong?" I asked.

"I've never been to a house party before. Well not unless you count Kirsty Gravens in sixth grade."

Chuckling under my breath, I placed my hand on his shoulder. "That's because you're weird and wonderful JimBob."

He smirked. "Yeah. I never had many friends before."

I smiled. "Well, you have now."

Natasha opened the door, inviting us both in. "What are you two waiting out there for?" she said, then eyed JimBob up and down.

Pushing JimBob forward, I smiled. "Come in. Come in!" she said, taking our hands and pulling us in further.

"Drinks are in there," she said, pointing to the kitchen. "But Layla… Lucas is in there." She smirked, nodding towards the living room. I groaned. She was always trying to set me up with somebody. "I'm sure he would love to see you." She laughed, pushing me towards the living room. I sighed. Hell. This acting normal thing was getting tedious. I found a seat on the sofa and began to survey the place. It's my own fault. I'd pushed myself to be popular, part of the in-crowd. But, with that came expectations. I'd gone from being a nobody to being a head cheerleader and number one on the Fuck list. I sighed. That bloody list! I should have stopped at Prom Queen, but no… I continued with the cheer leading, and now I have to continue with the whole charade. Mum and Dad were pleased though. I was as normal as normal could be!

JimBob handed me a drink then went over to make himself known. I'd pushed him to act normal too. He was currently dancing around some young girl I recognised from the year below me. The girl took one look at him and danced her way over to the other side of the room. JimBob shrugged and moved on to the next group. I smiled. Good for him.

I think the fact that he looked somewhat different scared people. I mean JimBob isn't your average eighteen-year-old. He was more than one of the goth types, way past emu and clashing with the rockers of the world. To be honest, I had no clue what he aimed to portray. But he was happy, and that's all that mattered. It's a shame that people don't give him a chance though. With all the loopy earrings, black hair, eyeliner, and whitened face. He was different. I guess a lot of people found that intimidating. But hey, let him be who he wants to be. Why should we all conform to what's expected of us? It's tiring to say the least. Still, it's a shame though. If that girl had given him the chance, she'd have found out he was quite a nice guy. One of the decent ones.

I always found it sad that people discern your personality based on what you look like. Mum had said we had to look normal, blend in a little, but stand out enough so that we could have eyes and ears everywhere. She was right, as usual. Being popular had its advantages. It meant I heard every bit of gossip out there.

I stood up, grabbed a few slices of pizza then sat back

on the sofa again. My friends always joked that I could eat like a pig but was still as skinny as a rake. Granted I was slim and athletic in build. I mean, I was a vampire hunter for Christ's sake. It kinda went with the territory. But God I loved my food. I mean, literally I ate plenty. I needed the calories. With all this extra strength and agility, it meant I burned through calories quicker than the average human. Heck. The last thing I wanted was to pass out in the middle of a battle. I frowned, finishing my pizza. Shit. Maybe that's what happened last night. Maybe I hadn't eaten enough. I did feel pretty weak when I went out. I know I wasn't ill or anything. It's rare we hunters ever become ill. But I'd been at the gym all day. Damn it. I should have eaten before I came out.

I sighed. I mean how was I supposed to take an original vampire out. The fact that the thought even crossed my mind last night shows how stupid I can be at times. I groaned, placing down the plate. Maybe I didn't have to do it on my own. Maybe my savior could give me a hand? I smirked. I mean, was that just me being stupid again? Mum and Dad had said not to trust him. What if he is working for Strauss and this is all part of some bigger plan? A way of taking down one of the five families in LA. Then again, why us? There were hunters all over the World. Why would he be interested in us? None of it made sense. I yawned, tired and withdrawn from the world. My body was still healing. I was lucky I'd survived. Too lucky maybe? I thought. Wondering if perhaps Mum and Dad were right after all? I sat watching the party play out before me, contemplating falling asleep on the sofa. But every time I closed my eyes, someone else came over and bothered me, talking about the usual crap from college, or the recent killings down by Club Neo. The whole serial killer talk had put everyone on edge and rightly so. At least this way, a few of these walking blood banks might stay home next Saturday night. One could only hope!

Either way, this side of LA was in good hands tonight. Steve and George were patrolling. They had been in the hunting business for years. All their family had. They had moved to LA when Steve married Josephine, they'd met back in high school, fallen in love and joined the two families together. Knowing the city was in safe hands, it put my mind at rest. Plus, it gave me and JimBob the chance to work out and start the training he needed. I was looking forward to the gym. I looked at my watch. It had been half an hour. Another half an hour and we could go. It wouldn't look rude then. I yawned, closing my eyes again.

CHAPTER SIX

Drifting off to sleep, I felt a hand grab my arm. Instinctively I grabbed it, twisted, and opened my eyes to a yelping JimBob. "Oops sorry!" I said, holding my hands up.

"No worries," he said, rubbing his wrist. "So, are we still going to the gym later?"

I nodded. "Yeah, give it another half an hour and we'll set off."

"Cool, so is your Dad out hunting tonight?"

"No, it's our night off. It's another of the families tonight."

"Another?"

I laughed. "Yeah, you didn't think we did it all, did you?"

"Well, I, erm…" he scratched his head.

I laughed again. "Go and have fun, then we'll head to the

gym."

JimBob nodded, smiled, and returned to dance with the rest of the party.

So, when I say gym, I mean the Honors gym, which is completely different. It was somewhere all hunters went to train, and I could guarantee Dylan would be there being as sleazy as ever. I barfed inside, swallowing back sick. He really turned my stomach. Plus, that dick had better leave JimBob alone. I could almost guarantee he'd try to make an example of him. Hmm. Maybe we shouldn't go tonight?

I looked over at JimBob. He'd be gutted if I said no. I pursed my lips. Sod it. Dylan can get stuffed. I'd take his perverted ass if I had to.

I hoped that with an immense amount of training JimBob would at least have half a chance against a normal vampire. I watched as he went over to another goth girl and danced beside her. She looked at him and smiled. Finally, he had found someone who would give him a chance. I guess in some respects, JimBob looked a little like a creep really. Dancing around the girls, hoping one will accept him. From an outside point of view, he looked quite scary. Like one of those people, you saw in the street and thought, he looks like he will be a psycho killer one day. I smirked. Maybe he will be good at killing vampires after all!

JimBob made eye contact from across the room and waved. I smiled, waving back, looking around the room. Why was I even here? This really isn't my scene. It was all for appearances sake. I sighed. I would love to be as ignorant as a normal girl, partying and clubbing late into the night. But when you know what I know, you can't relax wherever you are. I was always on alert, no matter where I was. Always checking out every angle, constantly casing the joint out. I smiled. I must have looked sad and lonely sitting there. But it's what I was used to. My brain was always on alert, checking out every part of the room, every aspect of the house. Vampires didn't need to ask permission to enter a home, it isn't like the old black and white movies, and vampires definitely did not sparkle. I grinned. The problem was, right now, this home was the perfect feeding ground.

I looked around the room. Three doors, two to the right, one beside the window I was sitting below. This wasn't the best place to sit, granted. But there were ample escape routes should anything go wrong. I'd even spotted the frying pan rack hanging from the ceiling in the kitchen. Hey, you never know what you're going to need to take down a vampire or two. I smirked. But realistically I was deadly serious. There could be any number of supernatural creatures in this room right now. Heck. The person sitting next to me could be one. There weren't just vampires in this world. There were demons, werewolves, and shapeshifters that I knew of. Luckily the wolves kept to themselves, living in country locations, so nothing we had to worry about, and demons, they were too busy bargaining for souls to give a shit about taking down any human in an unnatural way. Hell… if humans wanted to give up their soul for fame and fortune, who am I to stand in their way? Shape shifters on the other hand… they were nasty sons of bitches.

They could take the body of any person you ever loved, and you'd have no idea how to take them down. I mean Dad had only ever come across one in his lifetime, a young girl who nearly took Mum's life. But he got there just in time. Beheaded the body and thankfully never heard from the shifter again. I presume it's dead, but you can never really be sure.

I mean how is it possible that the body can morph and change, just like that. Shifting into another person. I mean, changing their molecular makeup and intermingling itself into what the hell it wants. Mirroring the person standing in front of them. How is that even possible? And do they have the person's memories too? Can they retain their habits, expressions, personality? How much of a shift do they actually make? I shook my head. I have no idea. This whole supernatural world was difficult to judge on the best of times. Especially today.

I knew Natasha's house well. I knew she had a side entrance, and in the back garden they had a gate into a back alleyway. There was a bike shed by one of the back fences in case we needed to jump over for any particular reason. And I also knew that her father was a Taekwondo instructor, so, in his office, which was through the door, straight on, from the living room; there were a variety of weapons, sitting there, ready for the taking. So, it was fine. Should any supernatural creature pop by and say hello, we had plenty to kick its arse.

JimBob had grown tired of dancing, swapped numbers with the goth chick and plonked himself down next to me.

"This socializing lark is quite hard," he said.

I laughed. "Yeah, it can be. People tend to automatically make their mind up by what someone looks like before they even give them a chance to speak."

JimBob gasped, placing his hand on his heart. "What, you mean I'm not as handsome as what I make myself out to be?"

I laughed. "Now, have you looked in the mirror recently?"

He grinned. "That's really not a nice thing to say to your work colleague, is it?"

We laughed. JimBob was cool. He knew what he wanted and didn't give a shit what anyone else thought. I respected him for that and was a tad jealous. After all, I couldn't go around wearing what I wanted, could I? Leather armor, kinky boots, and a stash of weapons on my back would get me arrested. No… it was jeans and a jumper with a concealed weapon or two. I had to look like a normal boring teenage college student. Well, seventeen-year-old, kind of still a teenager. Fitting in could be dull at times.

I watched college quarterback Lucas over the other side of the room, as two girls threw themselves around appearing more drunk than they clearly were. I laughed, motioning for JimBob to enjoy the view. He grinned and nodded.

I stood up, pulling JimBob up. "Right on that note, we need to get some training done."

We said our goodbyes to Natasha and our friends from college. Well, my friends from college, and headed off on the mile walk to the hunter's gym.

CHAPTER SEVEN

JimBob talked all the way to the gym. He was excited about being a vampire hunter. I sighed; I wish I could tell him it isn't as exciting as he made out. It's not like Buffy the Vampire Slayer. These were real nasty monstrosities. If you didn't have your wits about you, you'd be dead in a millisecond. One wrong move and your face would be crushed into a wall, your neck broken, and your body drained of blood. They were tough, strong, bloodthirsty creatures… well all except my sexy savior.

If anything, I felt for JimBob. He hadn't come across a nest yet. These broods were the worst of the worst. At first glance they appeared deadly, a hoard of evil coming in for the attack. But if you knew how, if you'd studied up before you leapt in, you'd know that their clans were easy to disperse. All it took was staking the leader and the sheep would wither away, turning to ash. You see, unlike Buffy; these vampires could be taken out by staking the sire. So, tactics were necessary, it wasn't just run in and stake as many as possible. It was a plan, practice, approach and eliminate. This is where teamwork came in, the five families coming together to annihilate the nest. I'd only ever come across one in my lifetime. An underground network created by a second level royal, one of the originals first turned vampires.

It was the first week on the job and I'd come across them by accident. Lucky for me, my Dad wasn't far behind. He'd pulled me out before I stepped into the nest without even realizing. It was that night, back then, that I realized I needed to learn everything there was to know about vampires.

I smiled listening to JimBob as he described the battle with a low-level vamp during last night's patrol. I nodded, grinning at his excitement.

We continued walking down the street, crossing the road, past Fletcher Gate and the Old-World bar. The music of the night swirled over the airwaves as the Doja Cats song, Woman, played out. Three women staggered out laughing and joking, heading past us to the next bar. JimBob stopped talking, watching them, smiling.

"They look like they've had a few!" he said, laughing.

I nodded and smirked.

The great clock in the center chimed nine times. Nine o clock, blimey, it was getting late, but we can still have a good few hours at the gym.

Jim Bob continued chatting away, as happy as ever. I stood on guard, watching every street corner, every darkened shadow. I know Strauss doesn't usually hunt on a Sunday. I'm presuming he takes a weeks' worth of victims in one night. After all, we'd had a fair few missing person reports lately. I'd seen the posters strewn around the college campus.

Out of the corner of my eye a figure escaped me. Jolting my head to the side, eyes narrowed, hands fisted ready for a fight, I waited. There was nothing there.

JimBob stopped beside me, he hadn't noticed. Instead, he continued talking, motioning the stabbing move with his hands, describing my Dad's kill last night. I'd laugh, but I was too busy watching the shadows. Was it a vampire, or something else? Were we being hunted? I huffed, then took a long, deep breath.

JimBob stopped dead in his tracks, eyes narrowed, watching me. I put my finger over my lips, quietening him to a standstill. Hairs on end, breathing slow, I was calm but on high alert. I'd played this gig a thousand times, I knew the drill. Panic and you're dead. It was that simple.

The wind blasted past us; a figure moved in the darkness.

"Show yourself," I said, my voice stern and resilient.

JimBob's eyes widened. "What, what is it?"

I reached beneath my coat, into the lining, pulling out a silvered blade from one of my Mums concealed pockets.

A figure stepped out from the shadows. Teeth gritted, eyes

narrowed, I stiffened up My feet naturally finding their battle stance, blade bared before me. Darkness silhouetted his face. He didn't pounce, didn't growl. In fact, his stature remained relaxed and at ease.

The scent of sandalwood aftershave caressed the air before me. I knew that scent. Knew him.

"Show yourself," I said again, my grip remaining tight on my blade.

Step by step his figure came into view. The face that remained in my memory appeared before me. The undead vampire I knew as my very own sexy savior… and I wasn't wrong. Hulking biceps folded across his chest as he grinned, fangs glinting in the moonlight. Silvered eyes swirled with an aura of oceanic blue. He stepped closer. Everything about him was predatory, his muscular body, dreamy face, enchanting aroma. He had invaded my thoughts and my dreams, and now my real life. This vampire was something different and no matter how hard I'd tried to stop thinking of him, he still showed up.

JimBob jumped in front of me, clearly distraught by my lustful panting and goo goo eyes. I smirked, snapping out of it.

"Get back!" JimBob yelled. His fists were up ready to fight.

The vampire smirked. "I am here for her."

"That's never gonna happen," JimBob said. His body shook as the vampire stepped closer.

I stood there, taken aback. Did JimBob realize he could

very well be signing his own death warrant right now? I'd better step in before this gets all out of hand.

"It's okay JimBob. This is the vampire from last night."

His eyes widened, "Strauss?"

I almost choked at hearing his name, "Jeez no! It's the vampire that helped me."

"Oh," he said, looking him up and down. "Well, I still don't trust him."

I nodded, smirking. "Me neither," I whispered.

"You do know I can hear you?" the vampire said.

"You were meant to," I said, smiling, flicking my hair. *Shit. Am I flirting? Damn, I'm flirting.* I scolded myself, straightening my back and standing firm.

The vampire stood before us. JimBob, by this point, had stepped aside.

"You shouldn't be out here alone at night," he said. His voice is soft and delicious.

My brow furrowed. Who does he think he is? He must know I'm a trained vampire hunter. I huffed. Surely, he should be the one that's afraid of me. My body stiffened. I stepped towards him, grimacing.

"You should know he has your scent by now."

I nodded. I knew. I was ignoring that minor detail. "He'll have more than my scent if he comes for me again."

The vampire smiled, baring his fangs. "Your arrogance will get you killed one day."

My eyes widened. Did he just call me arrogant?

Jim Bob stepped forward. "She's not arrogant. She's good at what she does now back off," he said, hands on his hips.

I smirked, as did the vampire. "I think she'll need more than your help," he said.

JimBobs bottom lip stuck out and he huffed, crossing his arms.

"I've been watching you for a while, Layla Stone," he said, licking his lips.

Shit. He knows my name. "You do know that makes you a stalker," I said, trying to remain edgy and calm. Inside my heart was pounding like a freight train.

"Or just protective."

JimBob frowned and pulled me behind him.

"I'm okay JimBob," I said, smiling and stepping to the side of him. He nodded, pouting.

"Why would you be protective of me?" I asked.

"Why wouldn't I?"

I bit my lower lip. He grinned, taking another step closer, until we were an arm's reach away. "You shouldn't be taunting Vampires Layla Stone."

My eyes widened. "Taunting? I rarely taunt my prey."

"Ah, so you think of me as your prey then?" he asked.

"Only if I want you to be." I smiled.

Stepping forward he reached out, caressing my cheekbone with his forefingers. Pulling my dark blond hair behind my ear.

I shuddered from his icy touch.

"There's something about you, Layla Stone."

I stepped forward so we were inches apart. "There's quite a lot about me, Vampire."

He smiled, sharp teeth glinting between his lips. "That's what I was hoping for."

"You were hoping for a stake in the chest?"

He laughed. "I was hoping for your help," he said.

My eyes widened. "Why on earth would I help you?"

"Because I helped you."

He had me there. He'd saved my ass. shit. My Dad would be pissed at this. I groaned. "So, what do you need?"

CHAPTER EIGHT

It didn't make sense. Why would an age-old vampire want my help, I was a hunter, I was trained to kill these things. I shook my head. Was he playing me? Trying to get me to lower my guard around him?

Taking a deep breath, I stared at him. No. The expression on his face told me he was serious. There's something different about him. Something almost human.

No matter how I felt about murdering the undead, I couldn't help but get this one out of my mind. It isn't just his goddamn gorgeous looks. It was his eyes, his deep solemn saddened eyes. This vampire had been around a long time. He had seen a lot, probably killed a lot too. It was right there in his eyes, the pain of the innocent lives he had taken. He buried it deep, kept it far far down, but I could see. Through this bravado was the sad, cold, traumatized undead life of a man that had no choice but to be who he had been turned in to.

I could almost understand that. I had been born into a life I never chose. I didn't have the choice but to live a life planned out for me, one where I made sandwiches by day, killed vampires by night. I'd never be rich, famous, or truly popular. No-one could ever know the real me. I'd be married off to the dick that was Dylan, be forced to have his vile children and continue the Hunter line throughout the ages. It was a shitty forecast, and one that I could see happening before it even did. I had no control of who I was, just like him.

As I studied him, he patiently awaited my reply. Looking into his swirling silver eyes, the deep blue of the ocean took me away. It gave life to the dead vampire that stood there, and there was one thing I knew, one thing that didn't make sense. This vampire, this one-of-a-kind vampire could feel pain. The sorrow inside of him was claustrophobic. I could sense it as soon as he had crossed paths with me.

It didn>t make sense though. This vampire, my vampire, could feel pain. I didn't understand how or why, but I knew he did. It's almost as though this vampire had a conscience, as though he had part of his humanity still intact. I shook my head. Was he ever truly a vampire, or was he somehow, Half and half? Half human, half that disgusting vile creature? Granted, it isn't a person>s fault when they succumbed to the bite of the undead. It isn't exactly a choice they were allowed to make. But to become one and remember and feel the agony you put your loved ones through is pure anguish in itself.

Remembering every kill, every scream, every man, woman, or child you bled dry. The horror of it would scar anyone that could feel.

When a new vampire is turned, he becomes rabid, taken over by a substantial thirst, a craving for blood, an unquenchable hunger. He would have experienced that. There's no way he could have stopped himself. The vampire instincts would have taken over and made him feed. I can guarantee he went home to his loved ones, unsure of what happened to him and why. He probably didn't even realize at first. I mean who knew vampires were real? It's only ever seen as a fable, or the trick of light as your mind captures something in the corner of your eye. You know it's there, but you can't quite see it.

This vampire, this caring, feeling, loving vampire would have seen the horror in the eyes of his loved ones, and there wouldn't have been a damn thing he could have done to stop it.

The normal vampires. The stinking, undead creeps of the night. They wouldn't care. To them humans were a way to end their endless hunger. They didn't give a shit about who they killed, why or when. A lot of them enjoyed watching their victims suffer through endless nights of torment; Strauss being one of them. No, normal vampires were just hungry. Carnivores and cannibals, dancing about in the world together. But still, none of them had a choice. This life was chosen for them.

In some respects, me being a hunter is finally putting them out there in eternal mystery. That's how I saw it anyway.

I smiled, looking deep into his eyes, and said, "So what do you want help with?"

He nodded and bared his teeth.

JimBob stood back and frowned. "You're not actually gonna help this thing are you Layla?"

I smiled, and nodded, "I kinda owe him JimBob."

He nodded and sighed. "But he's still a vampire, even if you do owe him, it ain't right." He kicked at the curb.

The vampire smiled. "I am not a thing. My name is Christian, Christian Livingston, and yes, I am a vampire. But as you have likely guessed by now, I am also much more. I am still human."

"Without a heartbeat," JimBob said, rolling his eyes.

"Indeed."

"Then you're not human," he said.

"Not in your mortal sense no. But I still do feel as you humans do. As I once did."

JimBob went to say something else, but I placed my hand on his arm and he quietened down.

"How?" I asked.

"How what? How do I still feel?" I nodded. "Honestly I do not know. I have always been this way ever since I was turned."

"But there is nothing of your kind in the Hunters history books."

"I kept myself to myself."

"Then why come out in the open now? Why save me?"

"Because I needed to save you Layla Stone."

"But why?"

"Because I need your help.

"With what?"

"I need your help to die."

My eyes widened; my jaw dropped. Did he just ask me to kill him? His smile dissipated. "I want you to help me kill the vampire that turned me, Layla."

"Why kill him? Why not just kill yourself if you want to die?"

"Because a vampire like Strauss should not be allowed to exist."

My eyes widened. "Strauss? Strauss turned you?" He nodded. "So, if we kill him, you will die too?" Christian nodded again. I smiled with sadness in my heart. I needed to kill Strauss, and Christian wanted to end his suffering, but I knew that with the deep tugging on my heartstrings, something inside of me would struggle to end Strauss and let Christian go.

I nodded reluctantly, but with one catch, we needed my parents to agree to the plan. After all, I lived in a family of hunters. They were my backup, they kept me safe.

He smiled. "Okay, but usually I'd ask a girl on a date before meeting her parents."

My cheeks flushed, which surprised me even more considering I rarely felt embarrassed.

JimBob huffed, grabbed my hand, and pulled me away. "Come on Layla, it's getting late. We'll go to the gym another day."

I nodded. What the heck just happened? Did he ask me on a date? Did an actual vampire fancy me, a human vampire hunter? What the fuck was wrong with this world. I rolled my eyes and quickly walked home, ready to begin another day.

CHAPTER NINE

18:30. My heart was pumping, head pounding, as though it could explode at any moment. What was I thinking, introducing a vampire to a vampire hunter? It was surely going to go wrong.

I didn't have much choice. Christian was going to go after Strauss, with or without me. And I hoped that my family's vengeance towards Strauss, would out-way their clear disgust of working with any vampire. Especially one that asked their daughter on a date last night.

I pursed my lips. Did he? I think he did. Jeez my heart was getting in the way of my head. What if everything was a ploy, a trick played out by Strauss? Could he have put all this together just to finish off our family? Would he? I laughed inside. Of course, he would. That sick asshole enjoys playing with his prey, and ever since that night, I'd become his next victim.

I carried on getting changed, armed to the teeth in hidden weapons… just in case. Plus, I knew Mum and Dad would be getting ready, just in case. Dad had demanded I kit up. He could be strict when he needs to be, but safety first. At the end of the day, Christian may feel like a human, look like a human, think like a human, but he was 100% dead as dead can be. He was a vampire and that's how my Dad saw it, no matter if he had saved my life or not.

Time ticked on. 18:45. Christian would be here soon and considering the fact that vampires didn't have to ask permission to enter, Dad had concealed weapons all over the house. Mum was watching the back door; Dad was at the front. He enjoyed the fact of having traps set, left right and center; and today I could understand why. Although I still felt Christian was the good guy. I mean, he was much more kind than most people I know, after all he did save my life. I can't say for sure that every person I know would have done the same. How many would have upped and ran, saving their own skin? Thinking about it, I could name at least a few.

Christian actually cared what humans thought and felt, and like he said, he felt every single thing that happened to him. He remembered every horrendous event; he'd put a mortal through. He couldn't help the fact that his only substance was blood, he needed it to survive, animals wouldn't sustain him. Eventually, he'd grow weak perish, shriveling into the ground he came from. No, vampires needed the blood of a fresh human. A fresh living breathing human, not just a little bit of blood either, but enough blood, nearly killing the victim in the process. The problem was the drinking, it was when their nature took over, frenzying, unable to stop.

The old grandfather clock chimed seven times, and with the seventh, there was a knock at the front door, every impact echoed through our home. The strength behind the knock was formidable.

I took a deep breath, walked out on to the landing and down the wooden stairs, step by step. Taking each step one at a time, unsure of the night ahead. The wooden steps creaked and crinkled, as the old house moaned and groaned. We'd had this place for centuries. It had been in the family passed down from generation to generation. The Stone family kept the property, because it was detached, set back against the woods, separate enough from reality. The last thing we needed were nosey neighbors. Our home was quite a large place, six bedrooms, the seventh turned into an office for Dad. An old workhouse out back with stables, a swing seat and the secret rose garden at the back of the property, through a wooden door behind a cascade of ivy. It reminded me of the one in the classic book; I'd imagined it as the very same when I was a child; especially with it being one of my favorite childhood stories.

I took the last three steps. Dad appeared in front of me and nodded, walking over, opening the door. Christian stood there and smiled. He looked almost human, except his pale skin, lack of breathing and invisible reflection.

But he isn't human. We know that, even if a normal

human wouldn't. Dad stood there rigid, eyeing him up and down, surveying the situation. I smiled at his three stakes in the back of his belt, the dagger in his hand and the umbrella stand with a sword, ax, and mace to hand.

This isn't just for our guest, this was home... and not exactly the house to bring friends home to. Although my best friends, the closest ones, thought my dad was some kind of a weird collector of weapons. I played on that, rolling my eyes when they bought it up.

Christian looked around my Dad to me and smiled. He opened his mouth to speak, but my dad beat him to it. "We have a lot to discuss," Dad said.

Christian nodded. "Yes," he said. His voice is smoky and mellifluous.

My Dad stepped aside, allowing him to enter.

"Hello Layla," he said, enchanting the airwaves, smiling as he entered.

This had to be the first time in a long time that a vampire had found his way into our property, and actually survived to tell the tale. It isn't the first granted, we'd had a fair few tries. They were usually decapitated by the time they got three steps into the home.

I smiled, watching him. Butterflies flutter in my stomach. I was giddy with excitement at him being here, right now, with me. He turned away and followed my Dad into the sitting room. I half-laughed at myself as I found myself staring at his bottom as he walked. Damn... I've got it bad!

While he was here though, while he was at least half-alive, I wanted to go on that date, get to know him, hold his ice-cold hand, feel his taste on my skin, his fangs caressing my neck. Biting my bottom lip, I took a deep breath and fanned myself down. I had to get a grip on myself, my hormones were running wild.

I thought back to last night. To when Christian confessed the pain he lived under. The trauma had eaten him alive; he simply could not cope with the anguish he felt any longer. I could tell he was weak, he hadn't eaten in a while. He hated every minute of being a vampire, but eventually he would succumb to his need to feed and kill another innocent soul.

I know he wanted to end his life, well, and his death. But I didn't want that for him. I felt there was something more to him, something that defied his kind. Evolution perhaps, had he taken a step up the ladder before the originals that walked before him?

I watched him walk away, wanting to take the final step and enter the lion's den with him. But I knew my Dad would make this hard on him, hard on me. I didn't want that. Nobody did. So, the longer I remained on this step, lost in a land of supernatural daydreams, the longer the reality of Christians final end stayed away.

CHAPTER TEN

Are you coming in?" Dad shouted, as I stood prized to the last step of the staircase. Christian smirked as I entered the room and sat down beside him. He was cool, composed and calculated. I on the other hand had invited a vampire back home and was awaiting my parents' permission. This was all kinda messed up.

My father remained standing glaring and Christian hands on his hips. His right-hand hovering over his stake. My knee began to shake, a vigorous ritual I used when anxiety would get the best of me. Christian sat comfortably, turned to face me, and placed his hand on top of my juddering knee.

"They'll be none of that here!" my father boomed.

Christian took his hand away and held them up in front of himself.

Dad narrowed his eyes as I sat back on the sofa. "So, my daughter tells me, you are a vampire."

Christian nodded. "Yet you feel like you did before you were turned." Christian nodded again. "Can you explain why you are different from all other vampires?"

"I wouldn't say I am different. However, my body did not appear to accept the vampire virus as well as all others."

Father sat down opposite us. "Explain."

"Well sir, I honestly do not know. All I know is that when Strauss turned me, I gained immortality, strength and the body of a vampire, but I also kept my human emotions."

"So, you also thirst for blood?"

"Yes, I can smell your daughter's blood from here."

"Gross," I said, frowning.

Christian looked at me and smirked. "Not like that," he said grinning.

"With the benefits of strength, agility and intellect. I also gained a craving for blood, a desire for pain and the pleasure through it. But through that came the remorse and guilt of hurting another human I ever murdered when I went into a frenzy." Christian lowered his head. "Their pin haunts me to this day. I cannot go on any longer. It has been centuries of torture. Both for humanity and for myself. "

Dad nodded, twirling the stake in his hand. "So why not ask us to stake you now?"

"Because I must stop Strauss from killing anymore people.

I need to make up for my past and that is one way I can try to do it."

"So, it was Strauss that turned you?"

Christian nodded. "Yes, I don't believe he meant to turn me. He simply did not drain me enough to kill me. Instead, he massacred my whole family, leaving me in agony as the change began to take place."

"What happened then?"

"Then after what felt like forever, I changed into the vampire you see before you."

"And what did you do?"

"I killed every person in my village."

I gasped. Dad looked at me. "And this is the vampire you trust to help us, Layla?"

I winced. Shit. He had a point.

Christian looked at me. "Hand to my heart, I will not hurt your daughter sir."

Dads' eyes narrowed. "Your heart isn't beating."

Christian smiled and nodded. "But the sentiment remains the same."

I sighed and turned to Christian. "Why me though? Why did you save me?"

"There is something unique about you Layla Stone, you have an aura about you."

"So, you saved me because you saw colours around me?"

He laughed. "No, I saved you because I felt warmth

around you. Somehow I knew you were different from all the rest."

"The rest of what?"

"Vampire hunters."

Dad coughed. "I mean no disrespect sir. But Layla is open minded. She gave me the chance to explain myself, rather than staking me at the first chance she had."

He nodded. "Yes, Layla has always been different." Mum walked in and smiled. "She takes after her mother." Mum came and sat on the arm of the chair beside me, stroking my hair.

"Err thanks mum," I said. Trying not to look weirded out by all this.

Dad sat forward, placing the stake beside him. "You do realize that when we kill Strauss, you will die too."

"I am counting on it."

"In fact, his whole bloodline perished with him."

Christian smiled. "It must be done."

"Fine. Then this week we will prepare for the upcoming battle. I suggest you say your goodbyes Christian and get any affairs into order."

Christian nodded.

"Then Layla, you will go with Christian to clear the area over the forthcoming evenings. But ensure you take your time. We will be on the radio if needed." I nodded. "It is only right that you get to finish the job you started." I smiled.

"That's all I want Dad, after what he did to me. What he

nearly did to me. If it wasn't for Christian, I wouldn't be here now."

Christian smiled. "I'm happy to help."

Dad nodded and stood up. "Layla, can I have a word in the other room?"

"Of course."

We entered the hallway stopping beside the front door. "Keep Christian in your sights at all times. Ensure he is always in front of you. He is still a vampire, and a bloodthirsty one at that."

I took a deep breath. "I will Dad."

Dad kissed my forehead and left for the evening. It was his turn to patrol, along with JimBob in tow.

Mum and Christian walked in.

"Thank you for your hospitality, Madam," Christian said, kissing her hand.

My eyes widened. "I'll walk you out Christian." He nodded. Mum took my coat off of the coat stand and wrapped it around me. "It's cold out there," she said. Kissing my forehead and walking away.

I opened the door, ushering Christian out.

"So how do you think that went?" he asked, as we stepped outside.

I smirked. "I think the fact that you're still here means it went well."

He laughed. "So tomorrow then?"

I nodded.

"I shall meet you here at sunset."

I smirked, "yes, and we shall go battle the beasts together."

He laughed. "Indeed, we shall." He nodded, smiled, and sped away into the night.

CHAPTER ELEVEN

After Christian left, I felt that a piece of me had left with him. When he was near, something inside me ticked a little bit louder. My stomach flipped, nerves ignited. JimBob would say I was crushing on him, and I sure was. But something more than my lustful teenage hormones bothered me. It was the sorrow deep down in his words. He carried the burden of every innocent person he had ever killed, and that alone is enough to destroy one's humanity. Yet somehow, Christians remained intact.

I sat beside my bedroom window staring out into the night sky. The old oak tree scraped its spindle fingers along the glass pane, wind hurtled across its remaining leaves, carrying the bright colours across the night sky. Autumn had passed and winter was in full form.

I can understand the emotional connection of killing an innocent person. I too had taken another's life. I was six years old, alone, scared and blinded by the darkness. Back then we owned a two up, two down town house in the back side of LA. It isn't the nicest of places, and something had awoken me that night.

Like always I had slept with a stake under my bed. Mum had always ensured we had a bag packed for emergencies, you know, a few cans of food, warm clothes, and that kind of thing. I'd added my brother's flip knife, he used to always carry it around with him. It made me feel safer.

So that night against the warm breeze of summer, I awoke cold in my bed. Nightmares of my brother's recent death had stirred me. Sitting upright I wiped the sweat from my brow and tried to turn the lamp on. It didn't work. In fact, none of the lights worked. Picking up the torch I had on my bedside, I rummaged in my bag and found the flip knife and stake. I knew I had to make it down the hallway to my Mum and Dad's room, but I remember the fear suffocating me as I stepped into the dark corridor alone.

Torchlights blasted through the house as two, maybe three people argued downstairs. I recognised one of the voices, my Mum.

Now my Mum was a hunter too, she could hold her own just as well as the next guy. But tonight, she was arguing rather than fighting. I tip-toed down the stairs, saw what I thought was a vampire launch itself at my mum and I ran as fast as my little legs could carry me. Jumping up onto the arm of the chair I flipped the blade out and stabbed the bastard in the neck.

Mum screamed. Dad hurtled down the stairs and picked me up, holding my head into his chest.

"It's okay Pumpkin," he said. "It's okay."

The other guy in the balaclava ran out the front door never to be seen again.

The next thing I know, Dad took me upstairs and the two of them called in reinforcements from the five families to help dispose of the body.

It was years later I found out the vampire I'd killed was in fact human. It never sat well with me after that. Dad said he was proud of me; I'd protected my Mum from the robbers. Whereas I knew Mum was capable of looking after herself. The reason she hadn't used violence that day, is because we have to keep a low profile. We can't be seen to be any different from anyone here in LA. I understand that now, but I still think back to the man I killed that fateful night.

Did he have a family, a wife, or a child? Had he turned to crime just to survive and feed them, so they didn't starve? Or was he really just another criminal looking for their next big score?

Whatever he was, I'd taken his life. That was the day I realized how strong I was, and I've never forgotten since.

So, I understand why Christian feels the way he does. Why he wants to end the suffering, the pain. But at the same time, that pain makes us who we are today. But with Christian he's stuck, in an endless time loop, never aging, never dying. Its torturous to say the least.

The thing is, the way I've got to see it, is that nobody chooses to be a vampire. It's something that happens one fateful night when you're walking home from a party, or you miss the last bus. When you take a shortcut through the alleyway, the dark, dank alleyway. Somethings lurking there in the shadows. And if that's something, that treacherous vampire doesn't kill you outright. If he leaves you still breathing. Then in time, you will turn into one of those, one of the vampires and join his horde.

Normally you wouldn't have any emotions. You wouldn't care about anything but the blood. Your loved ones would merely be your next meal, you'd go home and murder your whole town.

But if, like Christian, you had a conscience. It would be a torturous life to live.

I could see myself in Christian. I'd been handed a life that I did not choose. It was my birthright to be a hunter. To have the additional strength and agility to take down the monsters of this world.

I'd been able to see them. Seek them out. Take them down and save the innocent. But I had never had the choice. It was just the way it was. Both Christian and I were forced onto the paths we were taking.

Staring out of the window the night sky loomed overhead. It was getting late; Dad would be back soon, and it was time to turn in. Tomorrow was another day, the endless bore of the theory of physical education, as I knew I'd sit at the back of the class trying not to fall asleep. At least until my evening with Christian.

CHAPTER TWELVE

That evening Christian turned up a minute past sunset.

"Layla. Fancy seeing you here."

"This is my home Christian," I said as I stepped out onto the porch.

"Indeed." He grinned, his fangs glinting in the moonlight.

Shaking my head I put my hand forward, following my father's guidance. Keeping Christian in front of me at all times.

As we walked through the city, I watched him. Breathing in his scent, woody with a hint of whiskey trimming the edges. Perhaps blood isn't this vampire's only subsidence. I smirked. Had he needed a good ol' glass of Dutch courage before he stepped out from the shadows tonight? Then again, hadn't I?

Raiding Dad's liquor cabinet went well with the side

helping of a stake sandwich mum had made for me. Heck. I needed courage more than any hunter right now.

The problem I had wasn't the fact that Christian needed to be two steps in front at all times. The problem was that no matter where he stood, he could take me at any moment. I was starting to become drawn in by him. Not by the usual vampire charm. But something more. He was something more, and to me, he meant something.

I found myself speeding up. Coming side by side with Christian. Even though he had saved me, I was still cautious of him. But the distance isn't necessary.

"So, what did you do before you were a vampire?"

He smiled, gazing down into my eyes. "Would you believe me if I said that I owned my own estate?"

"Well, the clothing certainly suggests that?"

"What can I say… old habits, die hard!"

I laughed. "So do you always have a tipple of whiskey before you go hunting?"

He grinned. "No, but I do when I go out with a young lady I like."

Okay so my cheeks may have flushed at that comment. Damn. He likes me too. What in the world were we going to do?

"Well, err, thanks." He nodded. "Perhaps the outfit needs updating though."

He stopped, looked down at himself and smiled. "Fair

play my lady. It is a little dated."

"Just a little," I said, smirking.

"So, when this is all over, how about we go clothes shopping?" I said.

His expression saddened me. "I'm afraid that after all of this, I won't be around to accompany you to the clothes shops after all." He looked down at me, catching the watery eyes my body betrayed me.

I coughed, stood tall and nodded. "Yes. You will have your freedom from the burden of immortality."

He nodded, reached out and brushed his icy hand down the side of my cheek.

We continued walking, silent for the first few minutes.

"I understand you want to die to end the torment of the pain you feel. But what if there was a reason for you to keep living?"

He stopped again, took my hand, and held it to his non-beating heart. "It is not that I wish to die. It's that I'm already dead." I nodded, taking a deep breath. "I cannot continue to live like this when my survival depends on the death of others.

I lowered my hand, taking his in my own. "I wish there was another way."

"I do too," he said.

I took a deep breath and smiled. "It is strange having a conversation with an almost human / vampire."

He smiled back, "It is strange having a conversation with

a vampire hunter."

I smirked, as did he.

"So where do you want to go?" he asked.

My eyes widened. "Err, I was following you."

"No, this is all on you," he said.

I half huffed; half laughed. "So, you're telling me that we've been wandering aimlessly around the city streets of Los Angeles?"

"It would appear that way."

We both stopped walking, checking our surroundings. The night sky was calm tonight, the wind soft and cool. Street lamps blared out their bright white lights. Surrounding shadows danced with the trees. We had reached a local parkland, a place once filled with joy, during the daylight hours. At night, however, it was a place of unsolved murders. A location known for its vampire attacks over the past few months.

"So where do you think Strauss is tonight?" I asked, looking at Christian.

He stopped beside me. His hand brushed against mine. "Tonight, my lady, Strauss will be feasting on the blood of those he took before. He will be residing in the comfort of his own home."

"I don't suppose you know where that is, do you?"

"Sadly no. I have tried following him for the past few weeks, but he always disappears into this park, after that I do not know."

"So why did we really come here?" I asked, knowing full well every man had an agenda.

He grinned. "What better way to spend a Monday evening, than a walk through the beauty Los Angeles has to offer."

"Oh, so you were trying to get me alone. Were you?"

He smiled, his eyes twinkling. "I may have been."

I looked up at him. In those dark, charming, devilish eyes, his soul was kind and caring. My heart beat faster, as butterflies floated around my stomach. Dammit I liked him. How could I like him? Knowing what he was I've no idea. I shook my head. There was no reasoning to this rhyme. There was no explanation for my feelings. But I saw myself in him, the tortured soul; and with his devilishly good looks I felt an urge to be close to him, to hold one another and soothe the pain away. But he wanted to die to end it all to end the suffering but by doing so, by killing Strauss he would be gone. Removed from my life. The only vampire with a conscience.

He smiled. "Did you know that the old fair will be setting up here tomorrow?"

"I didn't know." I paused. "This isn't really the safest place for a fair."

"No, so perhaps we should attend?"

"I see." I said, smirking.

"What do you see?"

"You want to go on the Ferris wheel with me."

"I may do," he said, grinning. He took my hand. Ice cold

chills scampered up my arm. I shivered.

"Is it too cold? Am I too cold?"

I smiled and softly shook my head. "No, it's actually quite nice and refreshing."

He smiled and nodded. "So did you ever think you'd be holding the hand of a vampire?" he said as we continued walking through the park.

I laughed, "Well whatever you do, do not tell my parents."

"Ah, so I am not an appropriate suitor?"

"Heavens no!" We both burst out laughing, continuing our walk through the park and back towards my home.

"How do you think your parents would react to dating a vampire?"

I grinned. "So, are we dating now?"

"We could be, if you will take my hand and join me for an evening at the fair tomorrow."

I took his hand, smiled and he whipped me up into his arms, speeding me all the way home. The shrill of the wind captured my breath. I buried my face in his muscular chest, finding myself soothed in his arms, all the way home.

"Till tomorrow then," he said, as he placed me onto my porch.

I nodded. "Till tomorrow."

CHAPTER THIRTEEN

To say I had slept in was an understatement. It was already past eleven in the morning, and I'd missed my first class. Stretching out I sat myself upright and gazed out of the window. The sun streamed through; curtains left open. I vaguely remember my mother entering that morning, trying to wake me.

Beside me Jack Frost battered at the window. It was cold out there. Icy cold. But at least it didn't look like it was raining. Ah well. I may as well skip one day of classes and relax with a good book. Reading was my way of relaxing. Heck, I needed one, after all the hunting and normal teenage life I had to contend with.

Getting up I showered, dressed in tracksuit bottoms, jumper, and thick socks. It was damn cold in the house, even with the heating on. Grabbing a quick breakfast lunch, I headed back upstairs and sat myself down in the comfort of my egg chair beside the window. Staring outside I could see Old David Johnson back from his daily walk to fetch the newspaper. Martha Banatyne waved as she put the bin out, ready for the next day's bin collection. The world carried on as usual, unaware of the supernatural creatures living amongst them.

I sighed, picked up my latest Bella Day novel and snuggled up under my blanket. Turning the page, I continued. Laughing at the humor, smiling at the good bits, and softening when the boy meets girl, and they finally kiss. It was sweet, but nothing like real life. Well not my life anyway. I sighed, thinking of Christian. If only my love life was as simple as there's.

An old green Volvo pulled up outside. Dad was back. I knew he would moan at me about not spending the time preparing. Polishing weapons, sharpening swords, so I jumped up, closed the door, and kept quiet, snuggling back on my comfy seat. Right back to it. Another half an hour of reading and I'd venture downstairs, greet Dad, and make the family dinner ready for when Mum got home.

Christian would be here at six this evening, so I needed to plan what to wear. Granted, I knew I'd end up in jeans and a jumper, but a girl can dream. After all, it's too damn cold for a kinky black dress and high heels. Not that I'd ever be seen dead in them. I laughed to myself. I can't exactly take down a vampire now can I.

Placing the book down I went and got ready. A little make-up, tinted moisturizer, concealer and lip balm and I was ready to go. In fact, I might just add mascara, just to change things up a bit. Loosening my hair, I brushed it out, the waves of darkness curling around my pale face. I was ready, excited, nervous, but ready.

Christian met me on the porch, took my hand and smiled. "You've added something different," he said.

I grinned. "Mascara."

"Ah, well it looks exquisite."

Laughter escaped me. Dashing isn't a word I ever expected to be used alongside mascara.

We arrived at the parkland, the bright lights calling us in, enticing us with the music of laughter, love, and dance. It was beautiful. I hadn't been to a fair in what felt like forever. The last time was with my brother, before Strauss decimated our family.

It was the first night Beacon Fair had come to this side of the city, and with the ever-looming Strauss battle coming up. It was the last chance I had to enjoy my time with Christian, on our very first date. He'd asked for my hand, and I'd accepted. Little did he know I was an adrenaline junkie, and this was our last opportunity to share in the extreme adrenaline rush that came with gravity shifting through LA's cityscape. The

Gravity Shift was the ultimate ride, the one all the kids would die to have a go on; a Frisbee-shaped flying cocoon hanging delicately on a pendulum.

Its victims were pinned to the threshold, hanging on for their dear lives. It kept on spinning at miraculous speeds with the centrifugal force keeping the kids at bay. I looked at Christian, who held tight on my hand. Was it possible for a vampire to look paler than ever before? I smirked, looking at him. He was afraid and tried not to show it.

"Are you okay, Christian? You look paler than before," I asked.

"Yes, I will be fine," He said, smiling hesitantly. "Is this really what you want to do?"

"You only live once Christian!"

He laughed. "You only die once too."

"Ah good point, but I know you'll save me."

"Always." He grinned, taking my hand, and pulling me up to the ride, running towards the queue of future victims.

"Layla!" A high-pitched voice yelled. Natasha came running through the crowds.

"Ooo so who's this handsome man you've been hiding?"

I laughed, lifted my hand up, still holding his. "This is Christian."

Christian bowed. "A pleasure to meet you Natasha," he said.

"Oh, wow Layla, he's a keeper!"

I laughed.

"Are you going on the Gravity Shift, Layla?"

"Yes, we both are," I said, staring up at the monstrosity before me.

"Can I join?"

"Of course!" I exclaimed.

"Where's your friend?"

"Who? JimBob?"

She nodded. "He's out tonight."

"Ah shame," she said.

"Do I sense an inkling of curiosity there Natasha?"

"Maybe," she smirked, as we got on the ride. Christian held my hand tighter.

The wheel of doom started to spin. I was thrown into the hard metal backplate as it spun faster and faster, lifting, rising to the stars, cautioning that it could release us at any moment it liked. I screamed in delight, the freedom of the ride releasing me.

Christian strained forward against the force, gripping my hand. For the rest of the ride, I looked at him, smiled at him, with his wind-swept hair and tremendous strength.

The rest of the evening was spent together. Natasha took her leave and met up with another group of friends, leaving Christian and I to spend time together.

We walked through the fair, giving Christian time to get over his motion sickness. I laughed, he started to appear more human than a human right now.

Gripping my hand, he pulled me over to the water soaker. "Ah, you think it's funny, do you?"

I held my hands up. "What? That you, an immortal killing machine, feels sick on a fairground ride?"

He laughed with a sarcastic tone in his voice, then picked up a water soaker and chased me around the fair.

"Cut it out!" I yelled, already soaked from his perfect aim.

He sped past me, and I ran into him. It was like hitting a brick wall. Dazed, I stepped back. Placing down the water soaker he held me tight to his chest. "You've got to admit, that was funny!" he declared as I jabbed him in the side. He laughed again, sped off, then returned with a blanket.

"Where on earth did you get that from?"

"I have my sources," he said, grinning and wrapping it around me.

Drying off, we headed home. Him being the gentleman and speeding me all the way back.

CHAPTER FOURTEEN

"Good morning", I said, as I entered the Sandwich shop.

JimBob smirked. "Who got under your covers last night?"

I laughed and winked. Placing my coat and bag down and opening the blinds. The morning sun came streaming in through the front window, lighting up the gothic decor, old wooden tables and fancy artwork Mum had produced. She had created fake arches on each wall, turning the cafe into a setting for a horror movie, based in an old church. All we needed was pews, a half-dead ghastly nun and we'd be all set.

JimBob continued counting out the money in the till, setting the tables with dark purple napkins, sandwich menus and coasters.

I went into the kitchen and pulled out the sandwiches,

cakes, and cookies, filling up the refrigerated display cabinet in front of the counter. We had our routine in the mornings, JimBob and I, working together like two peas from the same pod.

Labeling the food in the cabinet I made a note of what we still needed and went into the kitchen to make more. It looks like the Devils Cupcakes were a hit yesterday. Luckily, Mum had made another batch of these last night. Besides that, I had to make more cheese, cut into the shape of an evil face. The younger kids loved them. Then there was tuna. We had a pot full of the stuff, brought in from Henry's Fishmongers across the other side of the city. I was yet to come up with a ghastly name for tuna sandwiches. I shrugged, spreading it on the bread. There just isn't anything frightful about them.

The bell dinged and JimBob walked in. Natasha followed. I smiled. "You do know we're not open for half an hour," I said, grinning. She always turned up every morning, before class to grab a coffee and a croissant.

"Ah well, you know me. I'm as keen as they come."

I laughed. "Anyway, don't you have class today?"

I shook my head. "Nope. Canceled for the next two weeks."

"Why?"

"Dillop broke his ankle while skydiving."

"Ouch!"

"Yeah, so Mum's put me to work here instead."

"Think of all the extra money."

I laughed. "One day, when I eventually get paid."

She smiled. "So, what's this JimBob tells me about you slutting around last night. Was it that fella I saw you with?"

I grinned. "It might be."

JimBob went pale. "What! Christian?" I nodded. "That's just wrong Layla!"

Natasha frowned, looking at him. "She's single, gorgeous and hot for it. It's far from wrong, JimBob!"

I laughed. "Well, he is kinda hot… but no, nothing happened." JimBob sighed in relief. "We just had fun, that's all."

"Well, whatever you did, it certainly put a smile on your face," she said, grinning.

Natasha picked up her coffee and croissant, hugged me and said her goodbyes. "See you on Saturday!" she said.

Huh? "Wait. What's happening on Saturday?"

"Err, we're meeting at the club."

JimBob looked at me. "Oh honey, that's next week," I said.

"Bugger, no problem. I can ask Jenny and Kate to join, then meet you next week?"

I sighed. "It'll be rubbish this week, Natasha. Why don't you go see that film you've been wanting to see for ages?"

"Oh yeah, that new one with Tom Holland?"

I nodded. "Good plan. He is kinda cute." I laughed. "Right, that's sorted then. But are you sure you can't meet us?"

"I'd love to. It's just Mum and Dad need me to help out, Saturday night. Apparently, we're having a few guests over."

"Oh, so not in the Sandwich Shop?"

"No, not Saturday. They're actually closing for the evening."

"Wow! They must be important guests then."

"Yeah." I shrugged. "I guess I'll find out Saturday."

She nodded. "Right, really got to go, else I'll be late. See you later."

"Okay honey, see you then." I smiled as she left, then turned to JimBob and widened my eyes.

"That was a close one," he said.

"Yeah. We don't want anyone near that club Saturday. Not if everything goes to plan."

He nodded. "So where will I be, Saturday night?"

"Well, if all goes well with the training. You'll be by my Dad's side. But that means staying glued to it," I said, laughing. "Strauss is not to be taken lightly."

"Yeah," he said, then gulped. "So," his eyes narrowed, "you and Christian. Are you a thing?"

"I, well, I don't know."

"I mean really, can he even get it up?"

"JimBob," I gasped, then burst out laughing.

"I'm being serious. How does it all work."

"God, you're bad!" I said, shoving him through the kitchen door.

Walking over to the front door, I changed the sign from closed, to open. Jerry came in, smiling away. He was always happy, relaxed and content with life. I always wondered what it would be like to be a Jerry.

"What would you like?"

"The usual," he said.

"JimBob, a Devil's wrap," I yelled.

"Extra blood," Jerry yelled.

I laughed, taking his money, and putting it in the cash register. He added a tip in the jar and went to take a seat.

The bell dinged again. Anne walked in. Anne was a fifty something year old writer, originally from Texas, with an accent that I absolutely loved. She would often tell me about the latest book she was writing. But most of them were crime or suspense, not my cup of tea. I'd had enough of serial killers in my time! "Morning Anne, what would you like?"

She smiled, her eyes lighting up at the display of savories before her. "I'll take a few of those pancakes, with a side of bacon please." I smiled and nodded.

"Coming right up," I said. Taking her money, I walked into the kitchen and noticed, she too had added to the tip jar. That's how I was paid here. Mum and Dad didn't need to give me anything for working here. The customers paid my wages.

JimBob smiled when I walked in. "Here's Jerry's Devil's wrap, with extra blood." I nodded, taking the wrap of bacon, egg and tomatoes with ketchup spilling out of it.

"Thanks, Anne wants…"

"Yes, I know. Pancakes with a side of bacon. I can hear you; you know."

Laughing, I left the kitchen and took Jerry's food over to him. Anne was seated beside the window, writing on her laptop. She often stayed for hours typing away.

Customer after customer came and went throughout the day. It'd been a long one. But one where I'd made a small fortune in tips, and when shared with JimBob, we came out with more than enough. JimBob was never happy about taking the tips, as he knew I didn't take a wage. But I told him it wouldn't be fair otherwise. Plus, I'd feel awful if he worked and only received minimum wage from my parents. He understood, but still wasn't keen on it.

Heading home, JimBob went to the gym to meet my Dad. He was out on patrol tonight. They both were. Thankfully I'd been taken off of patrol for most of the week. Mum insisted on me resting up before the big fight. Which I found strange, as I am sure the whole of the five families would be there at 10pm, when Strauss always shows. Either way, I didn't mind the time off. Relaxing in the bath with lavender candles, a good book and plenty of bubbles.

CHAPTER FIFTEEN

That evening was a cold one. Even with the heating on my bedroom still sent shivers down my spine. Training had finished and Dad was out taking JimBob into the real world. Granted, we didn't expect much tonight. Nothing much happened midweek. But vampires still have to eat. I shuddered. That meant Christian had to eat too. Burgh.

I'd agreed to meet Christian early Saturday evening, so we could comb the area and take out any potential threats. It was a good plan, but one I felt sad about. Saturday was just over a day away. It meant less time with Christian, and after our date I could see us both together. Okay so I know the dead thing might get in the way, but we'd find a way.

I sighed. That was until I turned old, wrinkled, and decrepit. I doubt he'd want to date me then. My body slumped down into my reading chair. I picked up my Bella Day book and continued reading. The audacity of this couple was compelling. He risked everything for her, nothing stood in his way. Whereas Dahlia played the hard-to-get card, using her womanly ways to entrap her husband to be. I smirked. I'm not sure I even knew how to use my womanly ways. But entrap, now that is something I can do.

Stretching out, I yawned. It was getting late and even with the hot cocoa Mum brought in, I was still struggling to keep my eyes open. Although, I expect that was the point. She clearly wanted me rested and at my best over the next few days.

Training had turned intense. Even Dylan, my sleazy future husband, or so he hoped; had struggled to keep up with the pace. We were pushing hard. Making sure we were ready to fight the one and only original vampire, Strauss. It wouldn't be easy, far from it. But the less casualties on our end the better. Unless it's Dylan. Perhaps I wouldn't cry so much if it were him. I smirked.

I stared out into the night sky. There was a storm coming. I could tell because of the splattering of heavy raindrops against my window pane. The oak trees' branches swayed, angry at the forthcoming winds, and with it I felt uneasy. The tides had changed, and something felt wrong. Fear crept up my backbone, as I stared outside. In the distance I could see one flashlight scattering its beam all over the place. Someone was there, and they were in trouble.

"MUM!" I yelled, jumping up and running down the stairs.

"I know. I feel it too."

"No. Mum, look!" I ran to the window and could see the faint silhouette of a person, dragging another person with them.

Running to the hallway I pulled on my boots and coat and ran outside. Mum followed. Coming up the street was my Dad, dragging only what I can presume is JimBob. I yelped as I ran, panting heavily. "DAD!" I yelled, running to help him.

"What on Earth happened?" Mum said, reaching us, helping to drag a very bloodied JimBob inside.

"Three of them," Dad said, between breaths.

Dad collapsed when we got inside. JimBob lay unconscious on the hallway carpet. Fresh blood tricked out from his head, absorbing into the fibers. JimBob's neck streamed blood. He'd been bitten and left alive. That only meant one thing.

"The bite!" I said, backing off, face paled.

"I know," Dad said. "I'm so sorry Layla."

I bit my lower lip to stop it trembling. JimBob's hand twitched, his body writhed, he groaned as his eyelids fluttered. He was coming too.

Salty tears fell as I scrambled forward and held JimBob's hand. "Careful," Mum said, wiping her own tears aside. "He could have turned." I nodded as Dad checked his teeth.

"Nothing yet."

"Maybe he'll be lucky," I said. "Like Christian was."

"I don't know honey," Mum said. "It's very unlikely."

"But we can wait, can't we?" I paused, the tears streaming faster. "We can see."

Dad sat beside me, stake in hand. "Layla, you know this is the last thing JimBob would want."

I nodded, taking a deep breath, curling my hands up to stop them shaking. JimBob would hate this. After his sister was killed, he vowed to take every last one of the blood suckers down. He even didn't like Christian. Despised everything there was about him. If we let him change into a vampire, he'd hate it. I gripped his hand tighter. Damn it! Why does this have to keep happening! I'm so sick of mourning the dead. They've taken too much from us. I clenched my fists, sweat beading on my brow. Sometimes we have to do the hard thing. Kneeling beside JimBob, I grabbed the stake out of Dad's hand and slammed it into JimBob's chest. JimBob groaned, withered away, and turned into a pile of ash. Dad looked shocked. But he was right. It was already too late. The process had begun and JimBob was lost to us the moment that creature bit him. What I did was mercy… but it didn't feel like it. Standing up, I brushed the ash from my hand and walked upstairs.

Mum watched, unspoken.

"I'll get the broom," Dad said, holding back the tears.

My body stiff, hands clenched, sweat beading on my brow, I was angry. Angry at the world we lived in. Angry that my one true best friend had been taken from me. He was the only person I could really be honest with. Who can I confide in now? Who can I take out and introduce to the world? How am

I supposed to tell everyone he's dead? I know we had cover stories. Run-aways, drug abuse, that kind of thing. But JimBob was neither. He looked like the typical goth druggie, but he isn't. Those that know him, know he isn't. What do I tell Natasha?

Dad had said to leave that to them. But I know she'll ask me. I know we'll have to come up with a believable story, considering there was no longer anybody left to find. It was messed up, all of it. How is it possible that I miss him already?

Entering my bedroom, I slumped on my bed and sobbed. Cried until my body could take no more and I slowly fell sound asleep.

CHAPTER SIXTEEN

Friday came. A day of mixed emotions. Anger. Fear. Grief. I couldn't get it together no matter how hard I tried. Blew off any plans for the day and spend the day in my room. It's not that I had any plans anymore. The person I'd planned them with, was dead. I could say I killed him. I did. But the logical part of me screamed otherwise. I'd killed the vampire taking over the corpse of my best friend. No matter which way I looked at it, or how guilty I felt that he died. It was not my fault. It was that vile creature that roamed the streets, and I was gearing up to find him.

From what Dad said, the vampire went by the name of Silver, because of the silver streak in his once brown hair. Apparently, Silver had come into contact with one of the demons and he'd paid the price for it. Like I gave a shit. I know Dad meant well though. He was trying to give me the background and prepare me for what I might face.

Dad wanted to come. But he couldn't. I wouldn't let him. He was still banged up from last night's disaster, and I couldn't risk losing him too. Anyway, he needed to rest for the forthcoming battle with Strauss tomorrow night. Shit. It's been a week already.

Mum had made me promise not to go alone. She'd encouraged me to contact sleazy Dylan. But even I wasn't that desperate. Instead, I had a feeling my one and only sexy savior was out on the hunt tonight, and if I made enough noise, he'd come calling.

So, that was the plan. Find Christian and take my anger out of the disgusting creature called Silver.

Armed to the teeth, I left the house. My parents were working, so this was it. Me out alone again, fighting the good fight. I didn't give a shit, what it was called. For me… this was revenge.

Making my way to the park, I saw the last of the fairground rides ride off on a lorry. I sighed. That had been a good night. If only I could go back, knowing what I know now, and stop JimBob and Dad from venturing out here back then.

With my back to a tree, I spotted a man walking alone. Now he could be walking his dog, or just out for a leisurely stroll, or he could be a vampire, dead set on draining me of all my blood. At this distance I couldn't tell.

"Yoo-hoo Mr," I said. Standing with my back to the tree,

weapons drawn behind my back. The man looked around and sped straight for me. Yep, that's a vampire all right. As he got close, I spun the stake around and aimed in front of me. The dick ran right into it, covering me in ash. Blowing away the remaining chargrilled skin dust, I scoured the area again.

It was a large park and would take me a good few hours to clear. Three dead ashen corpses later and I stopped for a drink. This staking business was hard work. Gulping down water, I reached in my backpack for an energy bar, unwrapped it and went to take a bite. From the woods beside me a streak of light blasted past, snatching my bar.

"Hmm, these are nice!" he said. Standing in front of me.

It was him. The vampire with the silver streak. "So, Layla Stone, what are you doing here?"

He knew my name. How the fuck did he know my name?

He laughed. "Strauss sends his regards."

Asshole. This vampire was in cohorts with the almighty. I looked around. Nothing. Then sighed with relief.

"Oh no, he's not out playing tonight. But take care princess, as this will be the last night you spend alive."

"Like fuck it is," I said. Launching forward, stake in hand. He dodged me just in-time.

Laughing he said, "what, you think I'd be that easy to catch?"

I growled under my breath.

"Your friend was. His blood was so sweet, skin so tender.

It was like breaking the hymen of a virgin all over again."

Launching forward I slipped, landing smack down on my stomach, in front of him. FUCK!

He knelt down. "Oh, my pretty, you're making it too easy!"

Gripping my hair, he pulled me up off the floor. I screamed. It damned well hurt!

There was no way I could reach him as he pulled me into his arms and held me tight. His teeth bared against my neck. "One little bite. I'm sure he won't mind one little bite."

I yelled. Summoning every last ounce of strength, I had. He had me trapped. My arms held against my body. But that wouldn't stop me. Wouldn't stop any hunter. It was a basic move we'd been taught as a child. Stomp, head butt, turn and stake. So, I did it. Stomped down on his foot, head butted him so hard my vision blurred. He let go and I turned, lifted my stake, and slammed it in the asshole's chest. His expression changed to one of pure shock as he stilled then turned to ash. I'd done it. Avenged JimBob's death, and tomorrow I'll avenge my brother's death. No matter what, or how, they will all die, once and for all.

The tree branches swayed as Christian sped through coming to my rescue. "A bit bloody late don't you think?" I asked, as he stopped beside me, staring at the pile of ash beside my feet.

"Clearly." He studied my face, Brought his hand up and caressed my cheek. His eyes solemn, saddened and concerned. "How are you doing?"

"Much better now he's dead."

He nodded. "Which one was it?"

"Silver."

"He was Strauss's right hand."

"Well, all the better dead then."

"Indeed. Would you care for me to take you home?"

I took a long, deep breath. "Yes, that would be nice. It's been a long night."

He nodded. Took my hand and whipped me up and into his arms, speeding me all the way back to the safety of my home.

CHAPTER SEVENTEEN

As the sun began to set, I sat on the front porch, five minutes, then ten. It was almost down below the skyline. An array of crimson, sweet orange and Sandy yellows caressed the ever-darkening sky. I sat there waiting. I knew tonight was the night. I'd hardly slept through Friday, paid minimal attention in class during the day and was too loved up after Thursday's date to make head nor tail of life right now. But today was Saturday. It was the day that I knew exactly where Strauss would be, and the night of which he'd be out on the hunt again, collecting his weekly victims.

The crisp wind bristled past me, my hair tied back, yet flowing in the breeze. I was geared up and ready for a fight. Leather trousers, boots, layered leather top with a jacket to match. Besides jeans, it was my go-to hunters' outfit. Every aspect had hidden pockets, blades and stakes tucked in anywhere they could go. My Mum had even made a pouch between my breasts, as a 'just in case' emergency pocket. I'd laughed when she made it, but now, now I was more than happy to carry as many weapons with me as I could realistically fit, without being encumbered.

The plan was for my sexy savior Christian to meet me after the sun sets. Then we are going to clear the surrounding area around Club Neo, lock the back door to the club. Okay so I know it's a fire door, but better to burn to death than walk out in the middle of a battle with the undead. I shrugged, smirking. Earlier on I'd secured a sword, two daggers and three stakes around the alleyway and behind the slip out the back.

Mum and Dad had arranged for the five families to get together, they were going to meet us there at 10pm; that was the earliest we'd ever seen Strauss, he usually waited for the early hours of the morning, when the drunkards were leaving the club.

Dad had already set off to go through their side of the plan with the other hunters. They are meeting over the other side of town below the library as usual. Mum held back to make sure I was safe, considering we all knew Strauss would make a beeline for me tonight. Christian had said that once he gets your scent, that's it.

The only other part of the plan was Christian. My one and only dead wannabe boyfriend. Granted I know, we hadn't gone past first base, but heck, I only met him a week ago. But still, I knew in my heart we were meant to be together. The problem is tonight isn't the night, and neither would tomorrow be, or the next day, or the next. I took a deep breath. I knew all week what tonight would mean. I'd lose him, he'd be gone forever, just like Strauss. Presuming the plan played out, when Strauss dies, Christian will cease to exist. The sky will be filled with thousands of ashen corpses, the wind taking their remains away to the netherworlds.

I'd lose him, and I knew that. I bit back the tears, shook myself and told myself to get a grip. He'd be here soon, and he couldn't see me crying over him. That'd be weird. Plus, hunters don't cry! We're made of strong stuff as Dad would say. We didn't have time to cry.

In the distance the trees swayed, leaves bustled and the blur of my one and only hope came rushing through the tree line.

"Layla," he said, his eyes narrowed as he watched me wipe my eyes.

"Hi Christian." I feigned a smile.

He took a step forward and sat beside me, taking my hand in his. "It will be okay," he said. His voice is soft and sensual.

I looked at him. "I know, and I know what we must do."

"But you are upset about something?" I lowered my head. "It's okay, you can tell me. I won't bite." He grinned.

I chuckled. "I know the plan, it's fine."

"Ah Layla, but that isn't it. Could it be that you're thinking the same way as I have been?"

I looked up; eyes widened. Did he like me too?

"Maybe." I smiled. "Maybe I don't want to lose you so soon."

He sighed; his eyes filled with sadness. "It is sad that when I find a reason to keep living, I must start dying."

Tears welled in my eyes.

He lifted my chin, looked deep into my eyes, and soothed away the tear that fell from me.

"Layla Stone, you are the light in my darkness. If only we had met sooner, we could have lived a life together. But the fates have another story to tell. You know this must happen." I nodded, he wiped another tear from me, and turned to face the woods before us. "We must be strong. Strauss cannot be allowed to continue killing anymore. I cannot continue killing anymore." I sighed, wiping my face, and leaning into his shoulder. "We will meet again, Layla Stone. Perhaps in another life, another romance. But I know in my heart, we will meet again."

I nodded, took a deep breath, and looked up at him. He turned to face me, our mouths inches apart. I bit my lip, looked him deep in the eyes and he kissed me. His cool skin caressed my warmth. Tongues searched deep, exploring one another, yearning for more.

The door behind us opened. Mum walked out and we pulled away, smiling at each other. Mum frowned. "Right. We need our heads on the game Layla. Are you ready?"

She had clearly decided now was not the time to discuss

our lustful desires.

I nodded and smiled. Christian smirked and mum walked back in the house tutting.

We laughed.

The wind blasted past as a shiver crawled up my spine. "Cold?" Christian asked, his eyes burrowing through me.

I nodded, pulling my coat tighter. He took off his jacket and hung it over my shoulders. I smiled, looking out at the starry night overhead.

Mum walked out, looked at me and frowned. "Right, I must go and meet your Dad. Are you going to start clearing the area?"

I nodded. "That's the plan."

Christian smiled. "I'll take good care of her, Mrs Stone.

Mum's eyes narrowed. "You had better do it," she said, grabbing her coat and closing the door behind her. "Phone us if you need anything, Layla."

"I will mum, don't worry. It's a good plan."

She took a deep breath, bent down, and kissed me on the forehead. "Be careful, I love you." And off she went.

CHAPTER EIGHTEEN

The first part of the plan was to clear out the surrounding area. We headed to the club and started in the vicinity, taking out Strauss's crew, one monster at a time. It was strange to see Christian in action. A vampire killing a vampire. Yet he was actually quite good at it. Tearing the heads off of each and every one of them. Stopping, he turned around, covered in blood. "What?" he asked.

"Nothing," I smirked.

"No, what?" he asked, closing the space between us. Our bodies touching, his hand lifting up my chin, his lips reaching down for my own. "What do you want, Layla Stone?"

I sighed, breaths escaping me. "You," I said, pulling him in for a deep bloody kiss.

He gripped me tight, searched my mouth with his tongue, groaned as we pulled one another close. Hitching my bottom up, carrying me in front of him. I wanted more. Needed more.

Then he pulled back, placing me down on the floor gently. "We can't," he said. I frowned. "We need to be alert; Strauss could come at any moment."

I nodded.

A shadow surfaced before us. "Strauss could come at any moment, you're right," a voice said, deep in the darkness. This was the voice of the killer I once met. The very same beast that took my brother away from me. I had almost lost my life to him. Trapped under his grip as he went in for the kill. Strauss was a sadistic asshole, and he was an hour early.

Christian darted in front of me.

"Oh my, Christian have you got yourself a girlfriend?" He taunted. Sneering as he looked past him, ogling my neck. "Don't worry I'll show her what a man looks like.

Speeding forward he bypassed Christian, grabbing hold of my collar, pulling me into him I kicked, flailing about, then heard the rasp of the material ripping. Bringing up my feet, I slammed them into him. Strauss hurtled backwards, right into Christians arms. The ground was cold, damp, and bare. The road was empty, and the only noise, the rock music from the club across the street. Two bouncers stood outside talking, oblivious to what was going on further down from them.

Picking myself up, I ran, stake in hand. Strauss flipped around, holding Christian before him. I banged into them, clattering to the floor. I clambered around, my stake unreachable. Instead, I found an empty beer bottle, smashed beside the railings. Picking it up, aiming for his face. He whipped aside, it caught his cheek, blood drawn, dripping down as he growled in anger.

His anger turned to manic laughter as he stepped towards me. "Oh princess, don't you think you ought to let the grownups play?"

I gritted my teeth, sprung forward and grabbed my stake. Knuckles white as I rammed it into his hand. He tried not to cry out from pain but backed off. I ran, jumped on the rail, then onto Strauss's back, grabbing him by the throat. I'd choke him, but it wouldn't make the slightest bit of difference.

Christian dusted himself off, sped away, took a stake out from my discarded backpack, and threw it at Strauss's chest. It impaled him. Strauss's eyes widened. "You missed it!" he yelled, laughing, taking it out and throwing it at Christian. The stake went straight through him. Two inches to the right and he'd be dead right now.

I gasped, curled my fingers into a fist and swung my body around to the front, smacking him square in the jaw.

He huffed. "You're quite the kinky one aren't you," he said, looking down, as I held on to him.

Holding tight, thighs wrapped around his body, I drew my stake and pushed in towards his chest. Fighting against his strength. Sweat beaded on my brow, palms clammy and heart racing.

"Oh princess, did you think it would be that easy?"

He gripped my thigh with his other hand, digging his long nails in. I yelped, loosening my grip. That was enough for Strauss to grab me and fling my body across the floor, like a ragdoll.

Back and forth we fought, until realizing Strauss was far from dead yet. Instead, I thought back to my training, pushing to act rather than react. Strauss found every one of my attempts puny in comparison, and Christian hadn't had much luck either. It almost seemed like Strauss enjoyed the combat.

Picking myself up off the ground again, I leapt in the air. Christian ran beside me, stake to hand, rushing to my aid. He lifted it and rammed it forward towards Strauss. Strauss pushed his hand away and pulled him close. "I always liked the taste of your blood," he said. Biting down on Christian's neck. Christian yelped, and I pulled him away. A chunk of his neck remained in Strauss's mouth.

"You will never taste my blood again," he yelled, speeding forward again. The two sped around the road in front of the club, jumping up walls, flipping over the cars. Strauss didn't care who or what saw him. A group of girls left the club, as two bouncers ran over to assist me.

"No!" I yelled, stay back.

Picking myself up off the floor, the bouncers kept running forward.

The first one, a red head with tanned skin and built like a tank, reached me first. "Are you okay Miss?"

"I'm fine, please keep everyone in the club."

"Why? You need help!"

"Please go!" I yelled. The other man with brown hair ran over, just in time for Strauss to reach him and behead him.

"GO!" I yelled. The brown-haired head rolled past me. The girls ran off screaming, while the other bouncer ran to the club and locked the doors.

Christians body flew past me, hurtling towards the entrance of the club. Strauss followed and I took my chance. Running forward I managed to throw a punch. My knuckle dusters doing all the work. Strauss saw blood again, his own, as it splattered the pavement. Grabbing his head, my fingers dug into his scalp. He isn't laughing now. Instead, I hurtled his body across the road, hitting a lamp post on the other side. He sat up, dazed. It appeared my strength even surprised me.

With my adrenaline surging and Christian by my side, we stood, battered, and bruised, but ready to fight some more.

Strauss stood up, brushing himself down. He half-laughed and half spat out blood. "You've got a good punch there princess."

"It's Layla to you." Eyes narrowed I pounced forward, he stepped aside just in time to grab me by the arm and snap it in two. Screaming I huddled to the side. My arm was broken. Shit. I need to place it before it starts healing. There was no time for that.

With the pain came the internal sound of my blood pumping, pounding through my ears. Salty tears fell as I tried to keep it together. It hurt. It bloody hurt. Wiping my eyes, the sweat and dirt blanketed them. It was dark. I was injured and Christian and I were no match for Strauss. Not alone. I needed my parents. The families. Watching Christian take on Strauss alone, I pulled out my phone, hit the dial button and left the phone on the floor, ringing my Dad.

"Hello Pumpkin, is everything okay?"

"DAD," I yelled. "HE'S HERE!"

I picked myself up, ran forward with my good arm carrying the stake and banged into Strauss, knocking him flying. Christian looked at me, assessing my broken arm. "Layla, you're hurt."

I nodded, wincing as I moved it. "It'll set soon," I said. He nodded.

"Until then, keep back."

I huffed, nodding, and wincing as I moved my arm to a better position.

Strauss walked forward, watching us. "You two are quite made for each other, aren't you?" He laughed. "After all, she hunts our kind for a living Christian. Did you really think she could ever accept someone as dark and deadly as you?"

Christian glared back.

"How would you know Strauss," I yelled. "Christian has more heart than you've ever had.

"Ah, but his heart doesn't beat. Or have you forgotten?"

I shook my head. "No, I haven't forgotten, but he is willing to sacrifice himself just to rid the world of you and your kind."

"Ah yes, of course. Your boyfriend will go up in smoke, won't he?" He laughed hysterically.

"Then let's get on with it, shall we." He grinned. Leaping forward past Christian and down on to me. I fell to the floor, trapped under his weight. "Oh, Layla, you're such an easy target."

"Get off her!" Christian yelled, pulling Strauss by the hair.

Strauss laughed, turned, and punched a hole through his gut. Christian fell to the floor, gurgling blood. He stood admiring his work as I screamed out, jumped up and staked him in the heart.

For a moment there Strauss laughed. Then he stopped. Looked down and saw the pointy end of the stake sticking out from his chest. Granted it may have been a cheap shot, stabbing him in the back, but I didn't give a crap right now.

As Strauss's body fell, it withered and turned to flakes or ash, floating away on the wind. He was no more, and with him every vampire of his lineage withered away into the dust they started as. Every vampire, except Christian.

CHAPTER NINETEEN

The night sky loomed high above. The moon threatened its very last phase. I knew sunrise was moments away, and there was nothing I could do to shield my love from it. He was too broken, cut up and destroyed. He couldn't move anymore and instead welcomed his fate as he soothed himself beside me, lying his head down on my knee, looking up into my eyes.

"It's okay Layla," he said, as I bit back the tears. "It's meant to be." I nodded. Christian turned to stare up at the morning sky as night time faded and the light of day began to show its fiery face. Still, the light around us dwindled, shadowing Christian's face. His pale features bled, sliced, and diced by the very creature that made him. A velocity of emotions saturated my mind. He was dying, just as Strauss did. If he hadn't stepped in, I'd be one of the fallen too.

Deep crimson blood pooled beside Christian's chest. My hand, covered in blood, pushed down on the worst of his stab wounds. I was puzzled over his injuries. As severe and deadly as they were, they were not healing. Nor had Christian turned to ash the moment Strauss was staked. For I knew Christian was a unique vampire, but to have these extra few final moments with him was a blessing. He lifted his head from my knee.

"Layla," he spoke, delicately pronouncing my name. "Why am I still here?"

I bit my lip. "I don't know Christian."

The dawn of a new day fielded the night sky. Rich crimson, vibrant orange, and the softness of yellow bled into one another, swirling, and twirling in a dance of delight.

Christian turned his head to the waning moon. "This is the perfect way to die," he said. My ability to hold back the tears ceased, as salty lips and a broken heart tried to piece my body back together.

"I will be with you Christian," I said. Watching the awe on his face as the sun rose for him, for the first time in over a century.

"It's exquisite. Like nothing I've ever seen before. My memory of the sun was shielded by the darkness." He paused and looked up at me. "Will you stay with me, Layla."

I nodded, wiping back the tears, stroking his hair, as his face brightened through the light surrounding us. I knew what this meant, I'd seen it happen before. Through the rays of the sun the dead shall burn. They always do.

A horde of footsteps pummeled the ground. Vibrations shook as the heavy boots of my Dad and the five families appeared around the corner. He looked over at me, and the pile of ash just meters behind. "Strauss," he said. I nodded. My face streaked through the pain of my upcoming loss.

As Dad looked over, he turned to see the sun rising, the light traveling over the ground, reaching us. He saw Christian, gurgling back the blood his body had lost, then he saw me.

"LAYLA! GET AWAY!" he screamed. I knew why. I knew the fire from Christians body would consume us both. But I couldn't leave him. Couldn't pull back and watch him burn alone. Something inside me pulled us together. A force beyond any other I knew. For in that moment as Dad ran towards me, the sun beam pushed forward, and Christians body lay still on my outlaid knee. He looked at me. Christian really and truly looked at me.

"I love you, Layla Stone," he said. I sobbed harder, closed my eyes, and felt the warmth of the sun encase my body. This was it. This was what burning alive felt like. A warm, magical feeling, like when you close your eyes on the beach and silence resides within you. A purified peace. A way to the Heavens as I felt uplifted and alive.

Wait. What. Why was I alive? Dad had pulled me up, releasing Christian from my arms as he saved me from the inferno.

Except there was no inferno. Just Christian, lying there in his own blood, surrounded by sunlight.

"Help him!" I yelled. Reaching out of my Dad's arms. He pulled me back, as my Mum bent down and soothed her fingers over Christian's face.

"He's warm!" Mum said.

Dad let go. "What?" He bent down; we both did.

As I touched Christian's arm, I could feel the reverse of death take over. A warmth traveled up his skin, color returned, humanity took hold "What's happening?" I asked.

Christian coughed out blood. I bent down, put my head to his chest and heard the first beat of his heart. The first breath as his chest rose and fell. The first pain, as Christian yelped. "It hurts!" he said.

"Get an ambulance," I cried.

"He's a vampire!" Dylan said, rushing up behind me. "No, listen!" I demanded. Dylan put his ear to Christian's chest.

"Shit man. His heart is beating."

"Not for long if you don't get help!"

He nodded. "It'll be quicker if we take him."

Dad agreed. The heads of each family lifted Christian up, placing him in the back seat of our car. "Quick," I yelled.

Dad jumped in, Mum in the passenger seat, and we sped off to the hospital.

Sat in the waiting room we were all covered in blood.

Dylan's father, Edward from the Rose family was easing things with the friendly police officers that turned up. After all, we all looked strapped up with swords and daggers, ready to take down half of LAs finest. The other four heads, my father included, were sitting at the side discussing what the hell just happened.

I walked over to join them. Dad looked at me. "Pumpkin give us a minute."

"No." I stated. "Christian is my boyfriend. I have every right to hear what you're discussing."

Dylan's ears perked up. "Your boyfriend? Gross."

"Not as gross of what you and I would have become." I said, flipping him the birdy.

"Fine." Dad said. "You may sit."

Edward spoke first. "Do you have any idea why he's human?" Dad shook his head. "This has never happened before."

"He was never fully a vampire," I said. "He kept his humanity when he turned." He nodded, and silence reigned over us all. Deep in thought Edward spoke again. "We must tell the others."

I groaned. I knew what that meant. Christian would be passed around as some kind of specimen.

"No." I said, sitting tall. "He will not be treated like a lab rat."

Dad sighed, then took my hand. "She's right. We can

access his blood from the records here. He needs to be left to get used to this life again."

I smiled.

The surgeon walked in, took aback by how much gore covered our clothes. "Err. Are you Christians family?"

I looked at Dad. Dad looked at Mum, then Dad said, "yes, we are."

"You may go and see him now. But beware he will be quite groggy from the anesthesia."

I nodded. Dad thanked the surgeon.

Entering Christians room was strange. Here lay the vampire, one that wore old-fashioned clothes, spoke well, and treated a lady as a lady. Instead, what I saw was a normal flesh coloured human in a hospital gown.

He smiled when he saw me. I returned the smile, ran over, and kissed him on the forehead. "You survived."

"I did, didn't I?"

"How?"

"I have no idea, Layla."

Pushing his hands on the mattress he began to push himself upright. Groaning at the pain, his right hand took hold of the handrail and he steadied himself pushing all his weight down to sit up properly. As he pushed, the metal cracked and creaked. Bending and breaking with his strength the handrail ruptured.

"What the heck?" Mum said, walking over.

Dad joined her, scratching his head.

I grinned. Took the metal handrail and bent it back into place. "You know what this means Dad," I said, looking at my father.

His eyes widened, he took a deep breath and said, "yes Pumpkin. It appears your boyfriend is a hunter."

The End.

Follow Layla and Christians next adventure in:

'The Devil Made Me Do It'

Pre-order available through Amazon.

Bio

Annalee Adams lives in England with her Husband, two children and a zoo worth of animals. She loves a good strong cup of tea or coffee, plenty of chocolate and binge watching her shows on Netflix.

Annalee began The Celestial Rose series while at University. She spent much of her childhood engrossed in fictional stories. Starting with teenage point horror books and moving up to the works of Stephen King and Dean Koontz. However, her all-time favourite book is Lewis Carroll's, Alice in Wonderland. Which explains her mindset quite well.

Connect with Annalee

Join Annalee on social media. She is regularly posting videos and updates for her next books on TikTok and Facebook. Join Annalee in her Facebook group:
Annalee Adams Bookworms & Bibliophiles.

Also, subscribe to Annalees newsletter for free books, sales, sneak previews and much more.
Subscribe here

TikTok: @author_annaleeadams
Website: www.AnnaleeAdams.com
Email: AuthorAnnaleeAdams@gmail.com
Twitter: https://twitter.com/AuthorAnnalee
Facebook: https://www.facebook.com/authorannaleeadams/

Printed in Great Britain
by Amazon